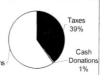

X Out of Wonderland

X Out of Wonderland

— A Saga —

David Allan Cates

STEERFORTH PRESS
HANOVER, NEW HAMPSHIRE

For information about permission to reproduce
selections from this book, write to:
Steerforth Press L.C., 25 Lebanon Street,
Hanover, New Hampshire 03755

Library of Congress Cataloging-in-Publication Data
Cates, David Allan.
  X out of Wonderland : a saga / David Allan Cates. — 1st ed.
     p.   cm.
  ISBN 1-58642-095-X (alk. paper)
  1. Optimism — Fiction. 2. Travelers — Fiction. 3. Social problems — Fiction.
  I. Title.
  PS3553.A84X26 2005
  813'.6–dc22

                              2005010194

FIRST EDITION

For my readers — friends and family —
whose interest made rain in the dry years

A truth ceases to be true when
more than one person believes it.

Oscar Wilde

Our hero's good home and fortune
and how he began to lose it

Not long ago, in the belly of a big-bellied land called Wonderland, there lived a young man who, in order to protect from unwanted commercial solicitations, we'll simply call X.

X grew up with loving parents in a prosperous time of peace. He attended public schools from kindergarten through the university, and after ten years in the building trades, he earned a graduate degree from the prestigious School of Ecology and Economics.

After graduate school, X remained at the university and became well known for his public radio show, *Home Renovation and Repair Issues.* He built himself a beautiful house in the country down a long driveway through a grove of Lombardi poplars. In those days the sky was mostly blue and the grass very green. There were brook trout in the creek and pretty horses in the neighboring pasture. X read of injustice and evil in the newspaper, and he saw it on the evening news, but, sitting on his water-sealed redwood deck in the evening after a day discussing with curious and energetic callers concrete slabs, vent spaces, blown-in cellulose, wall mold, and capillary flow through foundations, injustice and evil seemed far away indeed.

And for the most part, they were. X lived in a good country in a good time. His education taught him that Wonderland's abundance had not been accidental, but created by brave religious and economic refugees who, despite offensive Old World habits, such as massacring natives and importing slaves, had the genius and pluck to build the Global Free Market, an economic system that quite simply provided more food, shelter, medicine, and toys than all of the oppressive old gods put together.

So understandably, when X stood before the start of a ball game, facing the Wonderlandian flag and listening to the Wonderlandian national anthem, he often shivered with pride.

One night at a party, X met a tall African Wonderlandian woman with a hearty laugh and a big head of red hair, who he'd been told was a successful international private consultant. She walked over to him holding a tumbler full of brandy in one hand and a swizzle stick between the thumb and forefinger of her other. She stood a little too close for comfort and looked at him intensely through small dark eyes — looked down at him, actually, as she was taller, and she smiled strangely, and said, "Do you like jokes about white men with big cocks?"

X felt too flustered to answer. He knew it would be racist if he told jokes like this, but was it racist if she did?

She didn't wait for an answer. She licked her lips, leaned

a little closer, and told a dozen big white penis jokes, cracking up after each one. Even though X thought the jokes embarrassing, he couldn't help but like the woman for having such a great time telling them.

After the party he ran into her again, in the hotel parking lot. She stood with her big German Shepherd on a leash, apparently getting ready to walk home.

"You're gorgeous," he said, which is when he knew he'd drunk too much. He let his eyes drop from the woman to her dog.

"Who?" she said, "Seamus?"

"No, you," he said. He touched the dog's head. "I better go."

"Not so fast."

He paused and looked up at her, but couldn't hold her gaze.

"Why so shy?" she asked.

He shrugged. He wanted to lean closer and whisper something obscene, but he didn't know what to say. "Because I don't even remember your name," he said. "I'm sorry."

She looked more concerned than offended. "You should watch badgers."

"Why is that?"

She sat down on a bench, and the dog sat by her feet. "When a badger sinks its teeth into something, it hangs on."

"Is that right?"

"The badger is a beautiful animal," she said. "It's good medicine." As she spoke, she looked at him with narrow, unflinching eyes, as if she were dispensing life-giving, spiritual advice. "I told you my name once and you should have hung onto it. And since you didn't, you'll have to find it out again, and this time hold tightly."

"Let's take a walk," he said. And so they did, and the park smelled like newly mown grass. She let her dog off the leash and X took her hand and held it, and after walking for a while they sat down, the night air like cool velvet. X lay on his back and he felt her lie on her back next to him, their fingers still touching in the grass, and he looked up at the crescent moon, and suddenly remembered her name. He turned it carefully on his tongue like something sharp. It was a strange and beautiful name, African-ish, and its sound suggested the vulgar word for women's genitals. He whispered it but felt no acknowledgment from her, nothing in her fingers to show she'd heard. He said it louder, and still nothing. He sat up, looked down at her face, and realized she'd passed out.

He woke her — we'll call her C — and drove her home, where he learned she lived in a beautiful Tudor two-story separated from his home by only a half mile of oak and hickory forest. He walked her and her dog to the front door and watched her round bottom fill her dress as she bent forward to use her key, and he fantasized long berry-picking walks with her through the woods. In just the amount of time it took for her to open her door, step up, and turn to kiss him on the forehead, he imagined a year-long courtship, an engagement and marriage, followed by three or four multiethnic, multicultural children. She certainly had the hips for it! Happy and hopeful, X drove home to his well-lighted, cedar-sided split-level.

But things happening far away had already conspired to turn X's prospects inside out. A glut of wheat crackers and toothpicks on world markets had reduced prices and sent projected state revenues tumbling, so when X returned to work the following Monday his office was closed, and when he went to see the dean, he was handed a memo by her assistant stamped RECYCLE PLEASE across the top. The memo explained that because of a "bump" on the Global Free Market highway, his personal route to economic security now included a "detour." Small sacrifices would bring long-term prosperity to all, he was reminded, and "private" is always better than "public," so of course he would understand the decision to turn his department over to a large hardware store chain.

The FixIt Company would use its own personnel to do X's radio show, which was better because they could sell products while giving home improvement advice, and selling products meant more production, and more production meant more choice for consumers, and ultimately more wealth and jobs.

In his current state of unemployment, X had to agree that more jobs would certainly be good.

How the "downturn" got meteorological

That evening the faces on television who called their show *The Storm Team* showed weather satellite pictures, and the pictures showed "air masses." One of the air masses came from the north, the other came from the south, and they collided in the sky over where X lived, spawning tornados. One of the funnels touched down on X's home, splintering it to fragments the size of pencils, and then it carved a fifty-yard-wide swath of destruction through the forest to where it exploded C's house into similar-sized pieces.

X had been aware of the official tornado warning, and so had saved himself by hiding in the southwest corner of the basement as he'd been told to since he was a boy. C had not been listening to the news — she was bathing in bubbles — and the funnel sucked her out of the tub and up with a cloud of her home office papers and gently set her down, wet and naked, amid a snowstorm of falling receipts and invoices.

Climbing from the rubble of his home, X could think of her and only her, and he stumbled through the forest that was ravaged as if by a squadron of bombers. He found no trace of her, only thousands of pink papers with her name on the top, bills sent to businesses all over the globe for strategic services rendered, each for $187.36.

He searched the forest and the wreckage of her home, but he could not find her. The telephone lines were down, and his cell phone had lost its charge. Disoriented and sad, he wandered off in the direction of town, where he was directed to an emergency shelter set up for victims of the twister. There were cots in the high-school gymnasium, a line of people made sandwiches and served soup, and that evening the refugees sang and wept, and congratulated themselves on their strength and courage and good insurance policies.

Miraculously, C was in the shelter, too, dressed in too-tight donated clothing, and X gave her a comforting hug, and she gave him one back, and then they gave each other comforting kisses, and soon they'd stepped out of the crowded gymnasium and before long X had removed her too-tight donated clothing, and they gave each other many more comforting hugs and kisses. X told C about how he'd lost his job and offered sympathy for her destroyed home office, but C simply laughed and said oh well, she'd be all right, and she handed him a fat roll of cash. X thanked her profusely, with more hugs and kisses, and afterward, lying on their backs, looking up at the stars, X said he couldn't help but notice by the invoices strewn ankle deep in the ruins of her home that her business had gone global.

"Sure," she said. "I contracted an on-line bookkeeping firm to send out my bills, so I'll be getting checks for a long time. All I need is a P.O. box to live well."

7

X was dying to ask about her "strategic services," and why the charge was $187.36 on each bill, but she'd begun to kiss him again, and then she put her round bottom in a strategic place.

X tried to speak but made no intelligible sound, because C had begun to move in a strategic way.

The next morning X went to visit his insurance agent, a broad-shouldered meat-faced young ex-athlete who informed him that his insurance company had filed for bankruptcy just a few days ago when the economy burped, and so his claim would not be covered.

"I don't get a dime?" X asked.

"Nope," the insurance man said, "but keep in mind that the same government that killed the company with out-of-sight taxes is now stepping up to help the executives save the company and the jobs it provides, and the price of the stock will probably come up again eventually, so it's a pretty hot buy, if you have any spare chunks of cash to invest."

X agreed it would be a hot buy, but aside from the roll of 187 dollars that C had given him, he didn't have any spare chunks of cash. All of the extra money he'd earned from the radio job had been put into his house, so he was indeed destitute. The insurance man whistled through his teeth and said that was too bad, but sacrifices were required from time to time, belt tightening so to speak, and if and when X ever got back on his feet again, he should stop by and maybe they could do a little business.

"The key is that consumers like yourself don't lose

faith," the insurance man said. "Because this is one great country, you know what I mean?"

X did, of course.

Nevertheless, he left the insurance office feeling worried. Even though Wonderland was a great country, and even though these were the best of times, technologically speaking, and even though there had never been a system better at the delivery of goods than the Global Free Market, X still didn't have a home anymore, or a job.

Choice and Mobility, he reminded himself as he trudged along the sidewalk, his empty stomach grumbling, were twin virtues. And anybody who was hungry or homeless or without sufficient purchasing power, he knew, need not be so long as he or she chose to make the sacrifices necessary to move and retrain.

But his clothes looked ragged, he needed a bath and a shave, and when he got back from the insurance office the high-school gymnasium was packed with screaming teenagers, and technicians setting up cameras and lights to shoot a soft-drink commercial. All of the cots were gone. So were the soup servers, and, even worse, so was C. No note, no message, and despite the mass of people, no familiar face.

Uncertain of what to do next, X walked up the hill past the lime green water tower, then down through a muggy little park with a lot of old oak and walnut sagging in the sunlight. He passed an empty swimming pool behind a hurricane fence, and then a pink band shell. He wondered why all the invoices C had sent out were for the same amount of money, and he was impressed by the number of prestigious international companies she'd consulted for. He wished he'd saved one of the bills so he'd at least know her P.O. box.

He crossed the street to the sidewalk on the far side and walked by some children climbing a pipe fence that separated a hedge from the sidewalk. The homes were very nice in this part of town, brick with big front windows through which he could sometimes see wide rooms with mirrors on the walls, and the tops of stuffed chairs, and big color television screens. The driveways were smooth blacktop, and children rode trikes and bikes, or chased each other across the lawn and onto the sidewalk. The wind gusted, and X felt it cool the sweat on his neck and was suddenly exhilarated by the way the children's voices rose like leaves, swirled, and then fell into quiet again on the green grass. He waved, and a little girl straddling the fence was the first to notice. "Watch out for the homeless man!" she yelled, and all of the children scattered off the sidewalk, out of his way.

To keep from weeping, X breathed deeply, held the air in his lungs, and pretended he was watching himself walk across a movie screen. He was the star, and the camera followed him in slow motion, and he imagined grand and inspiring music. He was a man walking along the street of a small city on a hot summer day. A man who'd lost it all, and yet the Global Free Market and the country of Wonderland would provide. Something in his bearing, the tilt of his head, the length of his stride, or his ragged clothes suggested mystery and possibility to the casual onlooker, perhaps to someone in an upstairs bedroom of one of these houses who happened to glance out the window as he was passing, someone who just a few days ago had received good sound advice from him on vinyl-clad windows or stabilizing the wing walls of a basement walk-out.

At the end of the block stood a square, brick theater. He paused for a moment under the marquee, and would have pretended to be deciding whether he should enter, but the lobby was dark and where there might have been a movie poster behind glass there was only a sign saying No Loitering. Across the street a young woman stepped out of the Chinese-Szechwan Restaurant. She blinked, wobbled, and soon was joined by a lanky man wearing a tweed sport coat and Cleveland Indians baseball cap. Paper blew along the sidewalk from a tipped-over garbage can and then fanned out into the street. One of the papers blew up against X's shoe and stuck. X lifted his foot to get rid of the paper, but it wouldn't blow off. He shook his foot, but the paper merely wrapped itself around his ankle.

X bent down to peel it off and read:

An Economic Colloquium
Presented by Dr. Fingerdoo

A somewhat personal account of the history of the Global Free Market, emphasizing the role of Optimism and Positive

Thinking in the creation of Wealth and Prosperity. Although one might say the Consumer is blessed by a robust Economy, Dr. Fingerdoo makes the case that the opposite is true: The Economy is blessed by robust Consumers!

X took note of the time and place of the lecture. Dr. Fingerdoo had been one of his esteemed professors in graduate school. He folded the flier and slipped it into his pocket, then turned and entered the restaurant. One good thing about being jobless would be the opportunity to attend educational events.

X meets the boy and the woman in pink lamé, who has a car and a background in medieval history and retail sales

Green and orange paper lanterns clung to the walls just below the ceiling, giving the place an eerie, foreign look. The host frowned at X and began to lead him back through a narrow orange and green hallway into a roomful of laughing people seated around a long, T-shaped table. A couple of tables were not being used by this happy group, and one of them was occupied by an old man eating soup. X sat at the next table; the host gave him a menu and told him the waitress would be with him shortly. X looked around at the fifteen or twenty well-dressed folks surrounding the happy couple at the T-shaped table. An anniversary? No, a wedding. A fifty-something bride wearing a beige satin dress and pearl necklace sat next to the lucky groom, a man of similar age, tall and thin and handsome. X couldn't hear their conversation but felt washed by the music of their laughter.

"The groom's an asshole," grumbled the old man eating soup. "Look at that scrubbed face of his! He's an embezzler."

X, having fallen into a sentimental reverie about his and C's future wedding, didn't understand him. "What?"

The old man slurped soup from a spoon. "I've known him my whole life. He tucked away quite a nest egg in his first job as a bank accountant. He bought a beautiful house and lived there through twenty years of unhappy marriage."

"How do you know?" X whispered, embarrassed.

"Trust me," the old man said, and picked up the soup bowl to drink the last drops. He set it down again. "And before you go feeling sorry for the blushing bride, think again."

X didn't want to be in this conversation. He wanted to choose something from the menu, to get pleasure and nourishment from his food, and then to move on. Choice and Mobility! Nevertheless, he couldn't help sneaking a glance back at the bride.

"When she was seventeen," the old man said, "she ran away and did everything her narrow little mind had ever dreamed of. She partied hard, went a little bonkers, and hitchhiked a ride to the coast with a trucker. She thought she was free and the world was good, and then she got in with the wrong crowd one night and was raped and beaten and left for dead in a ditch. Even though she survived, she's never been close to a man since. She's been married three times, and three times she left her husband within a year."

X looked at her, at her pretty earrings and necklace and at the matching pearl buttons on the shoulder of her dress. He looked at her happy, shining face and watched her kiss the groom.

"They're going to be miserable," the old man said, and then laughed. "Within a year, the lonely groom will have come home drunk one too many times, he'll pass out, and the bride will shave his pubic hair! Then she'll leave."

The old man laughed hard and X lost his appetite. He decided that he didn't want to eat his meal amid such turmoil, so he got up and walked through another hallway toward the bar.

Inside the barroom, three walls were decorated by evenly spaced prints of ancient Chinese couples copulating in orchards and on the banks of creeks. The fourth wall was a folding plastic curtain on tracks, and on the other side of it an accordion band began to play a polka for the wedding dance.

Only two people sat at the bar: a young man wearing a Cleveland Indians baseball cap, and a vaguely familiar fat woman in a pink lamé dress who swayed her head to the music.

The bartender, a bald, thick-necked man with gray muttonchops, wiped his hands on a rag and eyed X suspiciously as he approached.

"What do you want?"

X wasn't sure where to start.

"Buy a drink," the boy said. "You get a hat."

"He doesn't need a hat!" the woman said from the end of the bar, her eyes closed, her chubby hands wrapped around her pink drink. "He needs to be certain. He needs to know how it will end. He needs cause and effect to be clear. And he'd like very much to find a woman for whom he cares deeply."

The bartender cracked a smile and looked at X from under his raised eyebrows. "Well?"

"How did she know?" X asked.

"She says that to everybody," the bartender said.

X climbed up onto a stool and rested his forearms on the bar. "Bring me a tapper and a shot, please."

A television hung on the wall behind the bar, above the bottles. Women wearing high heels and swimming suits, women who looked like no woman X had ever seen, took turns strolling across a stage.

"How come you look so ragged and dirty?" the boy asked. He was twenty, maybe, with short, dishwater blond hair, a freckled face. His feet hung down without touching the rungs on the barstool.

"I'm making a sacrifice for the economy," X said.

"Huh?"

"And I had some bad luck."

"I've had some of that," the woman said from the other side of him. She wasn't as fat as she had first appeared, just a little pudgy. Her eyes were closed, her eyelids colored an ugly pink to match her dress and drink. He noticed now that her head wasn't swaying to the music but was moving of its own accord, an involuntary twitch of some sort, as though she were saying a repeated No.

"I bet I know what you're thinking," the boy said.

X didn't answer. The bartender set a napkin in front of X and a full glass of beer on the napkin. Then he filled a shot glass with red whiskey.

"Sorry we're out of hats," he said, sliding the shot glass in next to the beer.

"Well?" the boy asked again. He'd moved a couple of stools closer, grinning broadly.

"Well, what?" X paid for the drinks with a couple of bills from his roll.

The boy eyed the cash and whispered, "You're thinking she must be some kind of freak. Admit it!"

The bartender pointed to the side of his head and made a stirring motion with his finger.

"You got a mind reader," X said to the bartender. "You could sell tickets."

"Sales are a cinch when you remember that *Homo industrialus* is a consuming machine," the woman said.

The boy squinted at her, his smile gone. "What did you call me?"

Behind the folding curtain on tracks, in the bar's outer room, the song ended and people cheered.

The boy asked the bartender, "Did she call me a homo?"

"Easy, big guy," the bartender said. "I don't like that kind of talk."

The woman in pink lamé opened her eyes, blinked a couple of times, then closed them again. She sipped her pink drink while continuing to move her head from side to side. Then she dabbed at the corner of her mouth with a napkin.

"I should have known better than to come to a place like this," the boy said, suddenly bitter. He sipped his beer.

Neither X nor the bartender nor the woman said anything, so he continued. "Ha! Dining and cocktails in an authentic Chink atmosphere!"

"You need Jesus in your heart, I think," the bartender said, and he pulled from his pocket various pamphlets he'd collected from sidewalk preachers. In one, Jesus offered peace. In another, he offered friendship. In another, the one with the color photograph of a little boy's laughing face, Jesus offered innocence and euphoria.

The boy fingered each pamphlet carefully.

"Pick a card, any card," the bartender said. "Whatever will bring you home, brother."

"What about bread?" the woman asked, also eyeing the Jesus cards. "What about mystery? What about authority?"

Suddenly the boy stood up and wandered over to the wall to look at the pictures. "I know what I need," he said.

"You need the fear of God," the bartender said to him.

The boy stood with his face about six inches from one of the ancient little obscene etchings. "I need Chinese pussy," he said.

"Language!" the bartender said.

"You need an elephant," the woman in pink lamé said, laughing.

X had downed the shot and was finishing his beer. Without any food in his stomach he felt instantly drunk. "I need a job," he said.

"Yeah, brother," the bartender said, pouring him another shot and beer.

X drank the second shot and felt the whiskey heat his face. "I need insurance I can count on. I need a good foundation. I need the right flooring, the correct roof pitch, and a mold-proof wall paint."

"Check out the new FixIt store," the bartender said. "They got everything."

"I need a decent ceiling vent, and shingles that won't curl in the heat."

"He has *enormous* needs," the woman said. "I find that attractive in a man."

The boy had moved down the row of prints, looking at each very closely. "I'll give the Chinks this much," he said. "They're a creative fucking bunch."

"Watch the potty mouth or you're outta here," the bartender said.

"I may be leaving soon anyway," the boy said, scratching his chin. "I may choose to go to Shanghai. I'm an artist."

"There's redemption in mobility," the woman said, laughing joyfully.

"And joy in sex!" the boy said, unjoyously.

The bartender made a sour face and shook his head.

"What I need is an heiress," the boy said. "A jelly donut heiress. A paper clip heiress. A grease zirc heiress."

"Grease zirc?" the woman said.

"The little grease nipples on machinery," X explained.

"Grease nipples?" The woman looked at him, impressed. "How did you know that?"

19

X shrugged.

"He inherited millions of them," the boy said. "A pile of grease nipples forty feet high! He's awaiting a call from a buyer."

"Maybe I can help." The woman pursed her lips, dipped her chin toward her shoulder, and said, "I'm currently unemployed, but my background is in medieval history and retail sales."

The boy had worked his way around the barroom and now sat back on his stool. "Sounds to me like she's a fucking expert in her fields," he said.

The bartender made a sour face and shook his head slowly as though disappointed again. He was mixing a new pink drink for the woman in pink lamé. "Language like that makes me feel filthy," he said. "This is an official warning. Next time and you're out."

The folding room divider slid open a couple of feet and two young men dressed in tuxedos walked into the barroom and disappeared into the men's room. X looked through the opening and saw the swirl of a beige wedding dress as the bride danced past. He listened to the polka and laughter and watched the bride through the narrow opening, long brown hair pulled high off her neck.

"Who's getting married?" the woman asked.

"Donny Darling's oldest girl," the bartender said. "And some guy from out of town."

"I'm from out of town," the boy said, smiling. "Maybe she's marrying me!"

"I like weddings," X said, thinking of his and C's, when

he finally found her. How far away could she be? It had been only a few days since he lay kissing her sweet cherry lips, holding her big head of red hair in his arms, and feeling her lovely bottom move. The music stopped.

"I went out of town once," the woman said. She fluttered her pink eyelids. X was struck by how familiar she looked, tried to remember where he'd seen her, and then decided it was in a cartoon.

"Yeah?" the boy said. "So what?"

"It was lovely," she said. "It was a lovely romantic weekend."

The boy snickered. Nobody spoke for a moment. The band started playing again and the room swelled with the sway of polka.

Then the boy said, "I had my first wet dream out of town."

The woman closed her eyes and laughed with pleasure. "Although the romance turned out poorly, I have no regrets. I need the freedom to make bad choices!"

"That you got," the bartender said.

"I was falling through space with my head clamped between a pair of thighs," the boy explained, squeezing his face with his hands and sticking out his tongue. "Falling and the wind all over my body like feathers. Falling toward a sky full of stars."

"Thank you for choosing to share that," the bartender said.

"We are not bored!" the woman said, raising her pink drink. "We are *not* not having a good time!" She drained her glass and set it down on the bar, her head wobbling. "Whew!"

X drank the rest of his beer. Betty Boop might be it, he thought. The woman looked like a grown-up Betty Boop. He looked up at the TV. A woman in a low-cut formal gown was being interviewed by a man. They stood on a stage, and four other women, also dressed formally, stood in a glass box behind them. A number, 4.74, appeared at the bottom of the screen when the woman finished answering.

"Turn it up, will you?" the boy said.

The bartender did and the boy put his face in his hands, elbows on the bar, and watched.

"You serve food at the bar?" X asked.

Without taking his eyes off the set, the bartender handed X a plastic menu with red tassels around the edge. He opened it and was about to order the Szechwan Chicken when he noticed the woman in pink lamé standing right behind him. He turned to see her face moving back and forth, but then she dropped her forehead onto his shoulder as though to steady it.

"I can see you're desperate," she whispered.

X felt her warmth on his shoulder. "I need a bath," he said. "I need new clothes. And I'm looking for a woman I've only barely begun to know."

The woman in pink lamé breathed excitedly against his neck. "I've got a car," she said.

X felt an electric thrill that seemed to lift him off his stool.

She took his hand. "Let's go."

Road trip, murder, hard time, freedom

Her car was a red convertible, and the boy came, too. They drove by the high-school gymnasium to look for C, but it was locked and dark and empty. So they drove past her old house to look for pink invoices with her P.O. box address, but the litter had been burned, the rubble bulldozed, and a little sign explained that the bare ground had been seeded in prairie grasses. So they drove to the store and bought some new clothes for X and then to a fast-food restaurant, and while the boy ordered a bagful of burgers, the woman in pink lamé took X into the ladies' room, locked the door, stripped him, and gave him a sponge bath with paper towels. X closed his eyes and imagined he was with C, which aroused him.

"Don't be embarrassed," she said. "I've scrubbed so many broken soldiers; I feel as if I must have been a war nurse in a past life."

"Broken?" X said, and opened his eyes long enough to peek down at himself.

"Inside, I mean," she said, and flicked him hard with her fingernail.

"Ouch!"

But X felt like a new person speeding down the highway, chomping burgers until his belly was full, wearing new clean clothes. The sun shone and the wind felt warm and the trees swayed in the breeze. The woman in pink lamé sat next to him, and the boy sat in the backseat. They were like a family taking a Sunday drive. The world sped by in an amazing show of prosperity. Attractively manicured lawns and gardens and fountains and odd sculptures suggested bounty. Store after store after store. Each full of an unfathomable variety of merchandise for unfathomable numbers of people. He passed a lake surrounded by giant houses, each with many windows.

"How lovely!" the woman said.

"And well built," X said. "I worked on some of them."

"What I don't get," the boy said, "is after you spend the first month fucking in each and every room, then what do you do?"

The woman in pink lamé giggled. "You're a pig but I like you."

X was driving very fast, and soon they were out of town. The green countryside lay before them all the way to the sky. They passed fecund fields thick with grain, lush forests, orchards heavy with fruit, and X was filled with a great optimism that came from the feel of the good car in his hands, the feel of the air on his face, and the magnificent ribbon of road stretching all the way to who knows where.

"Look at this highway!" he said. "Look at the bounty of this society and this economy!"

The boy snickered. The woman in pink lamé put her hand on X's thigh. "You're like the medieval peasant whose entire family has died of the plague but who knows God exists because once he walked all the way to Paris and saw Notre Dame!"

X moved his thigh out from under her hand, suddenly remembering how he used to have a nice house, but no longer did; used to have a good job and a woman he cared for deeply, but no longer did.

"Where are we going?" the boy asked.

"I don't know," X said.

"Uh-oh!" the woman in pink lamé said. "Now he's sad."

"No I'm not," X said. "I'm stubbornly optimistic. Because no matter how I might *feel* personally, it's a good system in the long run."

"*It? System? Long run?*" The boy laughed in the backseat. "If everything's so great, what are you doing with us?"

"What's wrong with *us*?" asked the woman in pink lamé.

The boy reached forward from the backseat and put one hand on each side of her doughy face to keep her head from its involuntary movements. "Nothing," he said.

Then he let her go, and again her head began to move back and forth.

"You're cruel," she said.

"I am," he said, "unfortunately."

A little cluster of black dots on the right side of the road grew in size and became two full-grown adult men wearing cowboy hats, boots, and large belt buckles. Hitchhikers.

"Stop," the boy said, "if you think everything is so great."

X slammed on the brakes, and the car came quickly to a halt. Two sullen cowboys slid into the backseat with the boy.

"Where are you going?" the skinny one asked.

"We don't know," X said, accelerating onto the highway again.

The even skinnier one pulled a very large revolver out of somewhere. "Well, then, let's do some consulting." He lifted the pistol to his ear and pretended to be listening. The boy giggled nervously. The woman in pink lamé's hand crept over and touched X's thigh again. The cowboy smiled, lowered the pistol, and pointed it at the back of X's head.

"*The border,* it says."

X tried to gulp down his fear, but it stuck in his throat. He couldn't speak.

"We're looking for our ma," the cowboy without the gun said. "Pa's dead and she up and left, so me and mah brother here are on a family pilgrimage. Ain't that right, Slimmer?"

"We do enjoy travel!" Slimmer said, and casually cocked the pistol with his thumb.

They drove all night across the big broad Wonderland continent, under a big broad sky, and to pass the time they took turns telling each other the sad and unfortunate turn of events that had led all of them to be in this car, speeding down the highway toward the border. Slim, the one without the gun, began: "We was born twins near the border. Pa sold shoes but drank up all the money so Ma started turning tricks and we did a lot better but Pa had this attitude problem. He took to cuffin' Ma and me ever'day, and humpin' little Slimmer here, and so one time Ah says to myself, Ah says, Slim, you bein' the biggest, you best not take this no more. And so the next day when Pa comes home all drunked up and commences on my brother here, Ah pulls out this here gun that Slimmer's got and tried to shoot him. Missed, but Pa left anyway. Bad thing is he took Slimmer and so Ah's all alone and grows up and goes to school and then don't go no more, and then Ah'm running with a bad crowd. Ah gets thrown in jail for burglary and murder and rape, and that was even a worse crowd. Been in jail since, until just last week, when my brother Slimmer here lawyers me out, and now here we are on the road, lookin' to find Ma, who Ah last seen twenty-some years ago lightin' a cigarette just as she ducked into a car with a one-legged foreign feller."

It was silent for while after he finished. Finally the woman in pink lamé said, "And after you and your father left, Mr. Slimmer, how did you spend your time?"

Slimmer cleared his throat. X wondered if the pistol was still cocked and aimed at the back of his head.

"Turns out Father quit drinking and did quite well with certain tech stocks," Slimmer began, "so we spent a good deal of time in Tuscany."

"Oh!" the woman in pink lamé said. "I've always wanted to go there! What's it like?"

"Well," Slimmer began, "the Tuscan landscape creates views of such poignancy that a drive like this can leave you feeling quite stunned. Take, for example, the tunnels one passes through on the way to Rome, which once entered make the landscape framed in the tunnel mouth appear as a miniature watercolor. As you drive, the picture slowly grows, until finally, bursting out of the tunnel mouth, you see before you a spectacular pastoral fresco."

"How breathtaking," said the woman in pink lamé.

"Indeed," said Slimmer. "When I last drove that route with Father, the landscape, or *paesaggista*, as the natives say, whispered the colors of springtime. In the valleys lay candy-green swaths of barley and wheat, and on the skirt of the hills a haze of budding *ulivi*. An areola of cypress circled the conical summits neatly capped with villas, terra-cotta nipples against an azure sky."

"Lemme guess," the boy said. "Pa may have found sobriety and a good financial adviser, but he was still humping you, right?"

"Sadly, yes," said Slimmer.

"And so you killed him?"

"I did," said Slimmer.

Again the car was quiet for a while.

"That's a good story," said the woman in pink lamé.

"But kind of downbeat, don't you think?" said X.

"He likes a good, chipper story," the boy said.

The woman in pink lamé took a deep breath and clasped her hands together in front of her with excitement. "May I tell my story?"

"Certainly," said Slimmer.

So she told about a long lonely childhood with no friends and no particular talent but reading history, and she told about her big sister's polio, and her brother running off when he was sixteen never to be seen again, and her mother's depression, and her father's post-traumatic stress disorder, and her hundred premarital lovers, none of them satisfying, all because of her jealous One True Love, which has turned out to be —

"Don't forget to mention your freak twitch!" the boy said from the backseat.

Slimmer reached across his brother and gave the boy a vicious blow across the face with the pistol barrel. The boy cowered.

"Don't interrupt," he said.

The woman, frightened by the sudden violence, said, "Oh, well, I was about finished anyway."

"But your One True Love?" Slimmer asked. "What is it?"

"Drunkenness," she said, and the car grew quiet.

"Okey-dokey," Slim said after a moment, turning to the boy, who was still holding his face. "Your turn."

The boy was whimpering into his hands.

Slimmer again reached across his brother, but this time he needed only to gently poke the pistol against the boy's head.

"Okay okay okay!" the boy said. And then told a story of privilege, of the best schools, of wealthy parents, of opportunity, of nothing bad ever happening, ever, except his favorite basketball team was screwed, absolutely screwed out of the state championship by bad officiating. Soon after that he left home and lived off a trust fund, and was looking for recreational opportunities when he stopped into the Chink restaurant for food and drink, and met the woman in pink lamé and the driver, X.

"Then we got in this car, and then we picked up you two fellows," he said. "Then one of you pulls out a gun, and then I have to listen to a bunch of blah blah blah, and then I try to make a little joke, and I get pistol-whipped. Now I'm forced to talk, and I don't even know how the story is going to end, because here I am, and the car is still moving, and so how do I end the story?"

"End it for him, Slimmer," said Slim.

So Slimmer pulled the trigger of the pistol and shot the boy in the head, filling the car with smoke and blood, and such a noise that for a moment X wondered if he himself had been shot. Slim reached across the boy, opened the car door, and pushed the boy out the door onto the highway moving by at eighty miles an hour. X watched the body of the boy bounce in the roadway, flip and flop, and finally come to rest on the grassy median strip.

"I reckon that's as good an end to his story as any," said Slim. Slimmer poked the pistol into the back of X's head. "Now your turn."

The dry lump in X's throat got drier and lumpier. "To die?" he managed.

"No," Slimmer said, "to talk."

So X told about his happy life, and then about his recent change of fortune, and then about how he was looking for a woman he cared deeply about, and how he was bound and determined to pull himself up again, and that he couldn't believe the Global Free Market wouldn't take care of him because he was just naturally optimistic, so that even though he'd just witnessed a murder and the car smelled of blood, he was feeling fairly good about his prospects in the long run because if he wasn't optimistic, then why not just drive the car right off a bridge?

Slimmer said, "I like everything about that story but the 'witnessed a murder part.' That part doesn't fit, aesthetically speaking. What do you think, Slim?"

Slim agreed. "Ah don't much care for that part neither, brother."

X felt the pistol push against the back of his head. His life story threatened to flash like a boring movie before his eyes. He said, "Okay, it's a lie! I just made up that murder part. I've never witnessed any crime in my life more serious than a parking violation."

"That's better," said Slimmer, and he pulled the pistol away from X's head. "Because frankly, I abhor violence, especially when it's used gratuitously in a story."

"Me too," Slim said.

After that the car was quiet for a long time. The sun set blood red, the sky darkened, and the cowboys fell asleep and began to snore. The woman in pink lamé moved a little closer and X could hear her weeping in the dark.

"He never found his recreational opportunities," she said. "He never found his heiress!"

"No," X said, feeling terrible.

The woman fussed with something in her purse. "At least I've got a little bottle of lime vodka," she said, and she passed it to X, who gulped twice and handed it back to her.

Suddenly he could see the immigration and customs buildings at the border ahead, and he expected that if he could pull in without the cowboys waking, the border guards would see the gun and arrest the twins and . . .

But what happened was this: When the cowboys were awakened by the customs officer, Slimmer quickly raised the pistol, pointed at X and the woman in pink lamé, and said, "We'd like to do our good Wonderlandian duty and turn in to you honorable officials a couple of suspected terrorists."

"Who suspects them?" asked the border guard.

"We do!" the brothers answered in unison.

So that's why X and the woman in pink lamé were handcuffed and hauled off to jail, while the immigration officer thanked the two brothers profusely and then asked how the blood got in the car. Slimmer said, "Oh yes, we were determined not to trouble you fellows with any complaints, but now that you ask, well, we used to be triplets, not twins, and the lady with the twitch wasted ol' Biff a while back, then dumped him out of the car."

The immigration officer showed great sympathy, embracing each of the twins, then each one again, and then the three of them compared guns, called each other patriots, and then embraced some more.

"Excuse us now," Slimmer said, "while my brother and I pass on to salve our grief on one of this tropical country's lovely talcum beaches."

The first morning in jail, X watched a South American boy get bullied during breakfast. Three young black men apparently had given him cigarettes, and he had not paid them back, so they surrounded him and acted as if they were real hungry and would he please share. He said sure and gave up his plate. But his tormentors accidentally on purpose threw the food back in his face. He was just a teenage boy and there was nothing he could do. He had to let them smash oatmeal in his face and then use his shoulders and hair for a napkin. The rest of the prisoners sat and watched the boy cry. They were all so afraid they could barely look at each other. But X couldn't endure it. He stood up and went over to the bullies and asked them to please stop. He acknowledged that this jail was a nasty place, and that historically black people had certainly suffered, but that was no reason to rub food on anybody. Incarceration had caused shortages and suffering for all, he explained, so in addition to staying well hydrated in this dreadfully dry cell, it was clear they also needed to stay confident and have faith that very soon the Global Free Market would improve everybody's prospects.

The three tormentors paused their use of the boy as a napkin. They stood openmouthed, listening, and when X finished his speech they took his head in their hands and pushed him forward and cracked it mercilessly against the table, *thump, thump, thump*, over and over again until he lost consciousness.

Later that day, X was led by a guard down a long hallway

to an isolation cell. On the way there he asked through swollen and bloody lips why he was being held.

"Because we're at war, you idiot," the guard answered.

"With whom?" X asked.

The guard laughed. "With terrorists!"

"But I'm not a terrorist," X said.

The guard shrugged. "It's a free country — you have your opinion, we have ours."

With that, the guard shoved him down concrete steps into a cold and dark cell and then slammed a steel door behind him. The woman in pink lamé had been thrown into another dungeon separated from his by a thick concrete wall. She went through an alcoholic withdrawal that caused her to scream like a crazy woman for three days, but when it ended she began to tap out messages on the concrete wall. In a code they invented, she described beautiful landscapes of orange trees and distant turquoise seas, and feasts of chicken and beef and pork and halibut and salmon and spongy chocolate cake, and cool mint ice cream, and aromatic Turkish coffee, and long and tender lovemaking sessions with a man she referred to only as The Lieutenant. The story seemed interminable, especially in code, but it made the long dreary days and the long rat-bitten nights bearable.

Then one day the woman in pink lamé's tapping stopped. X tried to start her up again by tapping out the last sentence that she'd tapped for him: "Down the sagging steps to the garden of lucky night, to Adam and Eve's quarter before the Fall, before there were words or music or presents to woo, or victories to impress, or pretty

34

poems or jewels with which to court, but only one scared covenant, the happy, happy, happy impaling of the woman on The Lieutenant's sensual staff . . ."

But he received no response. His filthy cell grew colder and lonelier, his only company death itself, always reposing in the shadows. His one distraction was to remember the cheerful afternoons he had spent at the hardware store familiarizing himself with products, the jolly fun of doing the radio show, and the relaxing evenings on his waterproof deck. Had it all been a dream? He remembered learning in school how the dream of Wonderland had been kept alive by suffering people everywhere, and so perhaps if it weren't for suffering people everywhere, Wonderland would not exist.

This made him optimistic, because judging by the groans and screams he heard coming from the other cells down the hall, there was certainly a lot of suffering going on. Also, he sometimes overheard the guards whisper to one another of their growing portfolios, so he knew the stock market was going up again. His blood surged with the expectation of freedom and prosperity and cleanliness, and he even dared to imagine C again, every inch of her flesh. When he slept, he'd dream that he was back on track with his career, and that C had moved in with him, and they were remodeling together for the new baby she was carrying in her pretty brown tummy.

Then one day the door to his cell opened and two burly guards smelling of cabbage grabbed him, handcuffed and blindfolded him, and dragged him up the stairs. "What's going on?" he managed to ask.

"The jail's been privatized and the care of prisoners has been outsourced to a facility across the border," a voice answered. "We're losing our jobs," said another.

A new guard took his arm and pushed him into a truck.

"What about the woman in pink lamé?" he managed to ask.

The new guard whispered something unintelligible in a pepper breath so foul it singed X's nose hairs.

The truck drove down a bumpy road for what seemed like hours, although X had lost all ability to judge time. He missed C, and the woman in pink lamé, and he even missed the boy and he didn't know why, just because he was a suspected terrorist, he had to be alone all the time. Finally the truck stopped, and he was taken out and led into a cool, coal-black cellar. He thought he was alone, but sometime during the night he felt the familiar nibble of rats on his feet. As hard as he tried, he couldn't keep from screaming. He screamed all night, until his voice had grown into something detached, an entity apart from him, and the pain and terror grew numb and distant, too.

In the morning, he was awakened, and the same guard with the foul pepper breath led him back up the stairs, mumbled something about cost-cutting measures, then opened a thick wooden door and pushed him out onto the hot and dusty street lined with adobe houses.

X blinked and rubbed his eyes. "Am I free?" he asked.

The guard kicked him hard on the bottom, which X interpreted as Yes.

The free market as a big fat sow

Miraculously, X still had some of the 187 dollars that C had given him. Feeling hungry, and hearing a commotion down the block and around the corner, he set off to find something to eat.

He turned the corner and saw a cloud of dust and a cluster of shanties and people that extended for blocks. The market! He felt happy to be here, happy to have money in his pocket, happy to finally be free to shop. He strode confidently down the street and entered into the mass of humanity and commodities. He passed huge piles of melons and apples and grapes. and barrels of rice and corn and beans and coffee, and he passed boys selling watches and necklaces and rings, and women selling brightly colored fabrics and feathers, and he passed men selling snake oil, barrels of oil, oil rights, and pictures of the cartoon character Olive Oyl. He passed recreational, miracle, and dangerous drugs, booths selling land lots and land rights, and rights-of-way, easements and ease. He passed all races and ages of men and women selling mythologies and the skeletons of their ancestors. He passed people selling memoirs, and the rights to publish memoirs, and the rights to sell the rights to sell memoirs, and sunglasses, and hundreds of plastic yellow ducks, and hammocks, baskets of frog legs, butterflies, and flowers. He passed blessings for sale, and curses for sale, and a man waving a smoking ball on a chain selling forgiveness. Thousands of eager young boys and girls stood scrubbed and combed, all for sale. A man sold tickets to a Dr. Fingerdoo lecture on Clitoral Economics, and a Dr. Fingerdoo lecture on Indian Scalps to Crack Cocaine: the Growth of Prosperity through Product Development. He passed men selling vials of sperm, woman selling ovum in petri dishes, and an old midget selling tacos. Despite his hunger, X moved on.

There were plenty of shoppers, too, hundreds and thousands of buyers shouting and reaching out their hands. Some wanted to buy hair. Some wanted to buy hair color. Many wanted sex secrets, investment secrets, or the secrets of happiness and sobriety. Some wanted lies and others wanted truth, and still others bought chicken soup in a can. Whole sections of the market were designated for ideas, both good and bad, whispered or shouted in hoarse voices by red-faced vendors. There were imitation-wood-grain products, and imitation crab, sapphires, vanilla, and musk. Large sections of the market were dedicated to imitations, others to originals, but X could see no clear line to show an eager consumer where one section ended and another began.

X passed long lines of people waiting to sell their souls so they could keep shopping, and even longer lines of those willing to betray someone for silver, as the price for betrayals has always been paid in silver.

The din swallowed X. He made his way fascinated and enchanted past naked chickens hanging upside down, dead pigs, live pigs, herds of horses, mules, and slaves. He paused by one of the slaves and asked, "Do you know where they sell burgers and fries?"

But the crowed moved him on before he got an answer. People shouted and grabbed and dangled shiny things in front of his eyes. The sun, the heat, the dust made him dizzy. An old man wearing a dead albatross around his neck tried to give away a very long poem but nobody wanted it.

"If he charged something," a passerby mumbled, "he'd have buyers!"

"Packaging's the problem," said another. "He's not attractive."

X passed booths selling products to fill your pock scars, to improve the shape of your nose, bottom, breasts, or penis. He stepped aside to avoid another man dangling a smoking ball on a chain selling the power to resist temptation and love your neighbor and live forever. A beautiful woman, half dressed, sold a song and a soft drink and a glimpse at her nipples. X passed piles of conches and pucca shells and sand and gravel and huge chunks of rock, and girls without hands selling diamonds, and guerrilla thugs selling the girls' hands, and other people sold the space in their bowels or vagina for carrying drugs, and others sold the skin of their face for kisses, and others sold a chance to throw a ball through a hoop, or a hoop over a bottle, or to throw a water balloon at a grinning parent, or a chance to throw a dart at a balloon, or to ride in a balloon, or to go to the moon, or a chance to see a freak of nature, or a chance to ride on a bicycle built for two, or in a rickshaw. Others simply sold chances.

A jumbo jet plane had been parked on the street, and a ticket agent sold tickets to any and all parts of the world served by air traffic.

"I love to travel," said a woman next to X.

Grateful to hear a human voice speaking to him, and only him, he turned, but the woman was gone. He turned the corner into a darker part of the market and passed a man with his abdomen slit open selling his organs, and a woman squatting to give birth to sell her baby. He passed the line for life insurance, car insurance, and university degrees. He passed football teams for sale, the players standing in the hot sun in their uniforms, their stadiums behind them, and then he turned another corner and he wandered past baskets of bombs that killed within a ten-foot radius, within a twenty-foot radius, within a hundred- and a thousand-foot radius. Bombs that burned their victims, bombs that blew the victims apart, bombs that sent chunks of jagged metal tearing through the victims' flesh. Bombs that killed everybody in the world except for the person who used it, and bombs that killed everybody including the person who used it, and also firecrackers and cherry bombs and ladyfingers, and poison gases and envelopes and paper clips and toxic compounds that removed rust from your car. He passed men and woman at attention with signs hanging from their necks, doctors, lawyers, generals, and eager young soldiers-for-rent standing in lines that stretched as far as the eye could see. He passed stacks and stacks of caskets, of flags. He passed baskets of newts and eyes of newts, and broomsticks and wands and household cleaning chemicals, and women with gnarled hands to use them. He passed clothing in every color for every part of the body, and for every sport or activity. Sailing outfits, and biking outfits, and soccer outfits, and jogging outfits, and shoes for hiking, and shoes for dancing, and shoes for cutting a deal. He passed undergarments for support, and undergarments for hygiene, and undergarments for seduction or incontinence. He passed moonbeams and sage and tangerine and moonbeams in jars, and sage in jars, and tangerines in cans. He passed people selling advice in all languages: on buying homes, on losing weight, on getting along with your mother-in-law, on your love life, sex life, past lives. Some people charged money to lay their hands on you, and others charged money to let you lay your hands on them. All X wanted was a burger and fries, and he knew he'd find them, but he didn't know if he'd die of starvation first.

Finally he turned another corner and there he saw a woman selling lime vodka. Her head was draped with a black cloth, but her head was moving back and forth, back and forth, so X couldn't resist stooping to look under her veil. Her pink eye shadow and Betty Boop eyes were unmistakable, as was the collar of her pink lamé dress poking up from under the veil. She recognized him, too, and they hugged and danced and kissed and hugged, and even through all the layers of his clothing and hers, he began to get aroused, he couldn't help it, and she pushed him away and said, "Let's be platonic friends, okay? I like to save sex for when I really really need something."

"Okay," X said, embarrassed, because he didn't want the woman in pink lamé for a lover. It's just that it had been a long time, and her soft body felt good.

"And besides," she said, "you're still looking for your gal, what's-her-name, right?"

X told her yes, of course.

"How did you find me?" she asked him.

"I was looking for something to eat," X said. "I felt dis-couraged, but I remembered something my mom always told me: 'There's something else around the corner, you bet!' So I came over here and hey, here you are! How'd you get out?"

"I was released on the condition that I perform 'good behavior' on some of the guards," she said. "They were just men, you know, they had their needs, and I needed to be free, so I took them up on their offer and here I am; sober, and back in sales, and working for myself, finally, and my foreign-language skills have improved significantly."

X pointed to the basket full of green lime-vodka bottles. "Are you making any money?"

She took his hand and guided it to a hard roll of some-thing between her breasts.

"Plenty!" the woman in pink lamé whispered. "There are no taxes!"

"Are there hamburgers?"

"We'll find something," the woman said.

And finally they did. There were lamb burgers and turkey burgers and buffalo burgers and pizza burgers, and burgers with every kind of cheese and topping, and finally, of course, just plain burgers. X asked for two of them from a pole-faced woman who took his money and handed him the burgers. He and the woman in pink lamé walked down the block and found a little park with a patch of grass and shade. While they ate, X chatted happily about his mother, the source of his optimism during the longest and darkest of his prison days.

"She told me once how she stayed up all night long on a mountain praying and singing. She watched the moon fade into the shadows of the night and the sun rise into the gift of a new day and she told me she was at peace knowing that although she was not at all good on the inside, and she'd never live up to her childhood dreams, that the Global Free Market as manifested in Wonderland loved her for who she was ever since the moment she was born into this world a baby consumer. Life is amazing in that although we can search the world and buy more consumer goods than we could ever use, there is always still a yearning inside us for more, isn't there?"

"That's beautiful," the woman in pink lamé said, dabbing a tear from her eye. And so they stood up and walked around the corner, and sure enough, there was something more, a cute little Persian restaurant, where the woman in pink lamé took X into the ladies' room, locked the door, and gave him a thorough paper-towel bath, and except for the occasional fingernail flick on his penis, he felt happy and good and lucky to have found his friend, who washed all of the dungeon dirt off him, then dressed him, and by this time they were hungry again, and so they found a window table and ate happily on and on until the sun set over the dusty free market.

The free market as a big fat sow that eats her farrow

The days turned into weeks, and the weeks turned into months and years, and X helped the woman in pink lamé sell the lime vodka, and they made a lot of money. They made so much money that they needed to do something with it besides stuff it in their pillows and mattresses, and under the floorboards of their little room, so they invested in plastic flowers and chopsticks, African gourd rattles, and artificially flavored beef. They made even more money as a result of these investments. The days went on, the buyers kept coming, and their platonic partnership grew stronger. Yet despite his success, X never forgot about C, and he always wondered where she was, and what she was doing, and who she might be consulting for. He tried not to think about whom she might be having sex with, but often wondered anyway.

X and the woman in pink lamé began to feel like an old married couple — packing up their wares and returning to their very comfortable condominium in the evening, he sitting on the couch doing a crossword puzzle, she getting an on-line M.B.A. They began to feel happy even, and X thought, What a great world, what an amazing world. He had money stuffed in his pockets, drawers and shoe boxes and cupboards, and they made investments in companies all the way across the marketplace, companies that they didn't even have time to visit, companies whose activities remained mysterious, companies that nevertheless sent them regular hunks of cash.

"It's great not to have any government regulation," X said.

In addition to selling goods and services, vendors in the market began to sell their entire booths to new buyers offering more money than many of the smaller vendors had ever seen in their long lives of toil. The new owners would often sell the product but not restock, then they'd sell the booth itself, the poles and sticks and nails, the pieces of black plastic and corrugated zinc, and sometimes they'd even sell the people running the booth, leaving only an empty space where the booth had been, and like this, the market began to feed on itself. The buyers of booths tried to buy our heroes' booths, but X and the woman in pink lamé chose not to sell and so they found themselves more and more isolated, with empty spaces growing around them. The swaths of empty space grew so big the wind and dust became a problem and the few customers who arrived at X and the woman in pink lamé's booths arrived tired, thirsty, and hungry, like intrepid travelers who had crossed a vast desert.

Then one day a one-eared man made his way to their booth and asked for a protection payment. They chose to pay him what he asked because they'd heard of others who had not, and who had suffered great losses.

"New people came and things changed," the woman in pink lamé said after the one-eared man left.

"What?" X didn't know what she was talking about.

"The history of the world in one sentence," the woman in pink lamé explained.

The man came back the next day and asked for more money, and they paid him that, too. A few days afterward, a ragged private army of ambitious thugs came through on horseback, and they demanded money and goods, and hay for their horses, so X and the woman in pink lamé gave all they could. The soldiers got drunk on the lime vodka and destroyed much of what they were supposed to protect. The next day they were gone, and X and the woman in pink lamé sighed deeply and rolled up their sleeves and rebuilt the booths. When they were finished, they were visited by agents for a civilian private security force who demanded payment to stand in the shadows and arrest suspicious-looking people. To prove how invaluable they were, the agents made a big show of beating and hauling off suspects and then dumping their tortured bodies on the edge of town where everybody could see them, or smell them, or at least notice the circling vultures.

In addition to assuring vendors of the need for security, this growing pile of dead suspicious-looking people often inflamed the brothers and sisters and cousins of the suspicious-looking people, so that these brothers and sisters and cousins sometimes strapped explosives around their middles and walked out into the crowded parts of the market and blew themselves and other shoppers and security personnel into uncountable body parts. As ugly as these attacks were, they actually made the security companies' profits grow by decreasing the troublesome crowds and increasing the merchants' need to pay for protection.

Soon no customers at all filled the wild spaces between vendors, only paid protectors. X and the woman in pink lamé still had some money coming in from one of their investments in a holding company, which apparently owned a number of private security firms. But what they paid for security was more than what they earned from this investment, and so finally one day the woman in pink lamé and X sat hungry and destitute on the street corner, no more vodka to sell, no more money left to pay for the right to sell it, and no extremely comfortable condominium. They could no longer pay for protection anymore, and so one night while X was urinating in an alley, he heard the screams of the woman in pink lamé as she was hauled off by professional thugs. "But I have an M.B.A.!" she shrieked. "I have an M.B.A.!"

X ran back around the corner to help, but she was gone. He passed the night frightened, sad, and hungry, and in the morning he joined a long line of forlorn and ragged economic refugees moving — *Mobility!* — down the street past armed guards through a great wrought-iron gate to a shoestring factory, where he would choose — *Choice!* — to work in dim light dipping countless shoestrings into an endless vat of dye.

Postmodern times and a dreamy reunion

The first morning passed interminably. As he stood on a yellow line painted on the concrete floor, belly to the vat, shoulder to shoulder with fellow employees, X's back ached, his feet ached, and conversation was impossible. In order to prevent chitchat, the company had arranged the employees so that no two standing next to each other spoke the same language.

WE BELIEVE IN A DIVERSE WORKFORCE! said a sign hanging over the middle of the factory floor.

His job was to dip shoelaces, one at a time, into the large vat of dye, then lift the shoelace and drape it over wires suspended above his head. Twice in the first hour he was beaten for not noticing that the shoestrings he dyed did not match one another. The beatings were administered to his knuckles with a large black garrote by a malformed boy who looked vaguely familiar.

He had to urinate but was told that he would have to wait until lunch break, during which time there was such a long line that he was called back to work before he had a chance to use the toilet. When he complained he was given five more whacks across the knuckles, which hurt so much he lost control of his bladder and had to work the rest of the day in urine-soaked pants.

That evening he was paid enough money to buy tortillas, beans, and pieces of plastic and cardboard to build a home on a nearby street filled with other plastic and cardboard homes. His fellow workers urged him to drink in the evening all of the water he'd need for the next twenty-four hours, which caused him to get up numerous times during the night to pee in the alley, but also allowed him to forgo drinking anything in the morning and so avoid repeating the first day's unpleasant disaster.

On the fifth day the workers on each side of X collapsed as they worked and lay motionless on the concrete floor. One was an old man who looked vaguely Asian, the other an Ethiopian girl of not more than ten. At first X was just going to keep working for fear he'd be beaten if he stopped, but some remnant of decency turned him away from the vat. He dried his stained hands on his apron and reached down to check each body for a pulse. None. Horrified, he stepped over the girl and off the yellow line and crossed the vast factory floor toward a carpeted tunnel that led to the offices of lower management.

"Come in and sit down," said a highly trained young personnel professional with nervous eyes.

X stepped into the office and did. The young executive folded his thin white fingers. X was transfixed by how smooth and white they were. His own were stained with dye.

"Two workers have died," X said. "They keeled over on either side of me. First one, then the other."

The young man breathed an audible sigh. "How terrible for you."

"Not for me," X said. "Terrible for the girl and the old man."

"Yes, of course." The young professional pursed his lips. "But at least their deaths will pay a benefit."

"A benefit?"

Before he spoke, the young professional took a deep breath, as if to reassure himself that it was for situations like this that he'd been trained.

"We insure all of our workers," the young man explained patiently. "The company is the beneficiary, and so by trickle-down coworkers also benefit. Would you like access to a grief counselor?"

X shook his head sadly. He didn't even know the dead people, which made him feel suddenly ashamed. How could he have stood right next to them for hours and days and have had no idea they were suffering so?

The young man made a small check on a piece of paper, then looked up at X, blank-faced, waiting. "Then what can I do for you?"

X cleared his throat. How could he begin to describe how in one short week, the hours and minutes of the day had become his enemy? How could he explain that when his two coworkers crumpled to the floor to close their eyes for the last time their faces — even the face of the little girl — had an expression of joyful resignation?

"The working environment is simply not humane!" he said.

The young man licked his lips and smiled condescendingly. "*Humane* is a cultural construct."

X remembered the little girl's face, her tiny, dye-stained fingers. He was trying not to cry.

"And *culture,* per se," the young man continued, "has done very little to help our customers gain access to cheaper goods."

X blinked, swallowed, and gathered his courage. The malformed, familiar-looking boy with the black garrote had quietly come into the office and now stood behind him.

"I mean," X said, "there's little light, no stools, and —" He stopped, ashamed of the tears brimming in his eyes.

"What you are lucky enough to be witnessing," the young man explained, "are the first tender, green shoots of the Global Free Market spreading into new territory."

"We can't even use the bathroom!" X said, and he knew his voice sounded like a pathetic whine.

Unable to hide his irritation, the young personnel officer sat back in the chair and sighed. "Listen," he tried again. "It is absolutely necessary for you workers to have the character required to keep your eyes on the big picture. Because if that isn't possible, I guarantee the factory will simply move across the globe to find heartier workers."

Suddenly ashamed at his lack of character, X stared at his own dye-stained fingers.

"In fact, we might move anyway. We could shut down tomorrow, and then where would you be?"

X remembered the filth of the shantytown where he slept, the miserable rain and the cry of hungry children, the drug-dealing wolves prowling the edges looking to eat the weak and the broken, the girls lining up to sell themselves as soon at they could throw on a cheap dress and skip to the nearest street corner — and also, of course, he remembered the woman in pink lamé hauled away as a vagrant by security. He nodded meekly.

The young executive smiled. "But just so you know we're not beasts, let me say I think you'll be pleasantly surprised by a change we have in store for you vat workers."

And with that, the malformed, familiar-looking boy with the black garrote led X out of the office and back to the line. The dead had been carried away; the spaces filled in with new workers. Before he left, the boy made a big show of giving X a quick flurry of stinging whacks across the back of the neck.

"Now don't leave your place again!"

The next day the factory smelled different. A chemical had been added to the vats of dye so that they gave off toxic fumes that made the world of the factory a dreamy place, made the pain in his feet, back, and bladder disappear. Even the occasional beatings became tolerable, and the days and weeks and months passed as if on a current of air. The fumes were so addictive that after only a few hours' sleep back in his plastic and cardboard shanty X woke with an insupportable craving to get back to work.

A year passed this way, and then two. X's eyesight was going bad, and he barely noticed the dull look on the faces of his fellow workers, some as young as seven or eight, others thirty or forty but looking eighty, and while he worked, he sometimes remembered his life in faraway Wonderland. He spent entire shifts remembering particular callers to his radio show, like Doc in Slinger, calling about a miraculous ten-year-old stain job. Or Bob in Lincoln, asking what kind of things he might be thinking about in regard to frost building up on his vinyl window casings. Or the man in Boscobel whose visiting lady friend created "quite a domestic issue" when she left spiked heel marks on his hardwood floor.

He also spent entire shifts picturing C's every feature. He spent a week on her flaming red hair alone. Another on her milk-chocolate skin, her neck, her shoulders . . .

Then one day he looked up from the vat of dye, up past the hanging lightbulbs and their rainbow halos, up onto a catwalk suspended high above the factory floor, and there, looking down on the acres and acres of workers dipping shoelaces into vats of dye, he saw her. He looked and blinked, certain it was a dream. Then he saw her tilt her head back and laugh. The sound came to him through his drugged senses clear and familiar, and then she turned and even from way down below he could see her round bottom filling her African-ish print skirt. He blinked and blinked again. He thought he must be fantasizing but nevertheless was pulled so thoroughly into the dream that he did something he hadn't done since his first week on the job. He pushed away from the vat, stepped off the yellow line, and despite the guards shouting at him, he climbed up the pipes onto the catwalk, where he noticed three guards down on one knee, their rifles aimed straight at him, and behind them, C's curious face.

Fearless as any dreamer, he said her name. He'd hung onto it like a badger after all, and her eyebrows went up and her eyes opened wide in recognition and her cherry-red lips moved when she told the guards to lower their guns. She ran to him, threw her arms around him, and he threw his around her, and they hugged and kissed and looked deeply into each other's eyes.

"Lover!" she said. "Gold hatted, high-bouncing lover!"

So they went into her office and hugged and kissed some more. He took her clothes off and she did all the things she'd done so long ago, and she still looked pretty, except a bit more wrinkled.

When they were done making love the first time, she stood up and clapped her hands twice, and yelled *Encore! Encore!* and so they fell into each other's arms again.

The second time they finished, C excused herself to go to the ladies' room and the malformed boy who'd done the beatings on the floor of the factory came into the office carrying tea.

The buzz from the dye fumes had worn off sufficiently so that X finally recognized him as the boy who'd been shot by Slimmer the cowboy and thrown out of the car. Or perhaps it was simply because the boy was wearing a Cleveland Indians baseball cap.

"You're alive!" X yelled, then went to him and hugged and kissed him, but the boy wriggled free and spat on him.

"Don't you recognize me?" X asked.

"Of course I do," the boy said. "I knew you from the first day you worked here. That's why I beat you so mercilessly. You drove on after that homo cowboy pushed me out of the car. You left me on the road to die."

"But he shot you in the head! I thought you were dead!"

"I was wounded, yes," the boy said, and he lifted his cap high enough to point to the large hole above his right eye. "But I crawled away. I was employed by a sensual products company that sold my sexual services to shy women. Because I'd broken so many bones when I was pushed from the car, I could contort myself into a small box and be shipped discreetly by mail. For a boy who likes to fornicate as much as I do, you'd think that would be the dream job, but you'd be amazed by what shy women require to get hot before penetration! I couldn't endure one more blushing female face describing to me her freaky fantasy! After a while all I could think was, Hey, what about me! What about my needs! So I escaped through a window one night and found work distributing fliers advertising Dr. Fingerdoo lectures. While making my rounds, I was often picked on by underemployed, low-income people. I was beaten and laughed at, and so I learned to focus my bitterness and rage and studied for certification to use this garrote here. It was about time I got practical. I earned top honors and pretty much had my pick of employment. Amazing the demand for a person who can mercilessly beat victims without leaving a scar! When I saw the benefits and stock options that came with this job, well, I jumped on it."

Reacquainted, relocated, reeducated

When C returned from the ladies' room she demanded to know why the boy was still there. X told her, and he watched her face cloud over.

"Well, go away now," she snapped at the malformed boy, who scurried out.

X was going to protest, but C put her arm around his shoulder and kissed him under his ear. "Just because I love you," she whispered in a voice that made him shiver with desire, "doesn't mean I care about every freak sadist you've ever known in the past."

They spent the afternoon getting reacquainted in her sumptuous office, drinking tea. X told her his story, and it made her weep, and so they stripped again and made love slowly, and then when they finished, she told him hers. She said she was at the spa getting a salt-glow oil massage when he'd come looking for her after the tornado shelter closed. For a while she wondered why she never saw him again after their "night of bliss," but then she figured he was a dog like most men. Anyway, she'd done all right. She raised her standard bill from $187.37 to $346.29 and it didn't seem to matter. So she raised it even higher, to $922.68, and still people paid!

"Why wouldn't they?" X asked. "Aren't bills *supposed* to be paid?"

C laughed again. What music! He was already fully in love with her again.

"But I never do any strategic consulting," she said.

"You don't?" X asked. "What do you do?"

"Nothing," she said. "I — or the computers — thank heavens for computers! — send bills randomly to companies all over the world. Thousands a month, and a certain percentage of companies pay. Who knows why? And who cares?" She went on to explain how the business made her fabulously rich, and so she'd invested in manufacturing facilities around the world, and this shoestring factory made so much money for her that she just had to come and see it. And so what a surprise and a coincidence and a miracle that in buying the factory she would also find him, her old lover boy!

She pinched X's cheek. The effects of fumes continued to wear off. He had a terrible headache. He said, "I'm addicted, and I'm going to go through withdrawal, and I'm going to beg to be put down on the line again, but please ignore me. Just lock me in a padded room for three days and no matter what I say, don't let me out."

So that's what C did. And for three tortuous days X suffered a magnificent hell in which all the great battles of the Civil War were fought in his skull. His brain grew so big it exploded, and then it shrunk, and he had to pull his hair to keep his skull from collapsing. Caissons rolled, troops marched, rifles fired, and when he finally emerged from the padded room, great handfuls of his hair were missing.

But he was sober, his eyes clear, and the slaves were free.

C had been preparing to go back to corporate headquarters, and X was to go with her. Because he didn't want to leave the malformed boy behind again, he waited until C was post-orgasmic, when she was the most carefree and kind, and then asked if the malformed boy might accompany them on the company jet. She answered as if she'd never said anything cruel about the boy in her life. "Why not? Of course! Your friends are mine!"

Then X thought about his fellow workers on the factory floor and wondered what he could do to help them. He was afraid to go down there for fear he'd get high again. And he didn't really have any friends, as he'd never spoken with his vat mates. Still, he'd never forgotten the faces of the old man and the girl who died next to him, and he knew there were hundreds of suffering people working on the floor, and so he walked out of C's office onto the catwalk to look down and try to figure how he might help. But when he stood high above the factory floor, when he saw the dye-filled troughs extending like red, yellow, and blue ribbons almost as far as the eye could see, when he saw all the workers bellied up to the vats, their hands moving in a blur, when he saw the row after row of hanging shoelaces drying on wires, the whole scene seemed the creation of an artistic genius. Trucks bringing material from the far corners of the globe delivered at the dock while other trucks picked up the packaged shoelaces and carried them back again to the far corners of the globe. He squinted down and tried to focus on the individual worker, tried to imagine the mountain or seaside village where he or she came from, tried to imagine what had driven him or her away to this place. A tornado? A local economic "adjustment"? Famine? He thought of the giant lighted words CHOICE! and MOBILITY! hanging over the protected shantytown where most of these workers spent their nights, the squalid jumble of plastic and cardboard from which emerged nightmare screams, whimpers of dying children, and the groan of a mother's grief. He tried to remember the ubiquitous shit smell, the hunger and terror, but the scene on the factory floor spread so undeniably grand and beautiful below him, and his clothes felt so clean and soft, and his body so rested, and his stomach so full, that it was almost impossible to imagine it ever being otherwise.

Bladder pain, foot pain, back pain? Those ailments seemed puny in comparison to his current good health and the scene of endless production below.

Lost in reverie, he didn't hear C approach. He smelled her clove cigarette, though, and knew she was standing behind him, next to him.

"A penny for your thoughts," she whispered.

X didn't know how to begin. He pried his eyes away from the magnificent sight of the factory floor, the beauty and unfathomable scope. He lifted them until they came to rest on C's cinnamon cheeks and lively eyes.

"My life without you was like a bad dream," he said.

"Well, now you're awake," she said. "And a limo is waiting."

They flew back to a city on the coast of Wonderland in C's private jet. While the malformed boy crabwalked back and forth, grumbling about how his garrote had been taken away for the duration of the flight, X and C spent the long hours making love in the back bedroom.

At corporate headquarters, a giant white building of the most modern design with carpeted hallways leading up, down, and sideways, X was given an office next to the malformed boy's in the Management Suite Campus. From out his window he could see groups of employees lying around or playing Frisbee out on the Great Lawn, or eating happily at the outdoor French Bistro cafeteria. They all made comfortable salaries being creative and had tidy stock-option retirement packages. Clusters of accountants with tongue studs and pirate bandanas played Hacky Sack while inventing flexible measurements to better interpret the company's fabulous growth. He watched Dr. Fingerdoo himself, surrounded by an entourage of highly trained economists wearing long purple robes, stroll across the lawn holding forth. His lips shone with spittle and his brow creased. He used sharp hand movements, graphs, and sometimes moving PowerPoint presentations to bolster his arguments for increased investor confidence.

Publicly, C showed the required reverence for Dr. Fingerdoo and his cohorts, but privately she scoffed at the economists' explanations for her success.

"I only keep them around for the benefit of the stock-holders, who for some reason can't accept that success and failure are mysteries. People like to think the universe is rational and metes out wealth according to merit or reason."

They were sitting in a restaurant eating. It was their hobby, eating in restaurants. It gave them a good, multicultural feeling to taste flavors from all over the world while listening to music from all over the world and being waited on by people from all over the world.

"They say risk, sacrifice, and hard work drive our economy," she said. "But it's been my experience that the people who talk most about those things are really talking about somebody else's risk, sacrifice, and hard work!"

X nodded. "They also talk about Investor and Consumer Confidence."

"Holy Ghosts," C said. She shook her lovely red hair and laughed joyfully. "Anybody who thinks she deserves her good fortune is a fool."

"And bad fortune?"

"What about it?" She took a bite of roasted goat, chewed it carefully.

X told her about the old man and the girl who died next to him on the factory floor.

C shrugged and swallowed. "Bad fortune is simply bad fortune. There's nothing any of us can do about it."

X swallowed and felt his face flush. He shivered as a light breeze touched the colorful flags along the veranda. "You can't really mean that," he said.

C opened her eyes wide and leaned across the table. She spoke very carefully and precisely: "I'm a descendant of slaves brought to Wonderland in chains and starving peasants, their mouths stained green from trying to eat grass. Personally, I try not to suffer, but the world seems to require it. If I believed it would help, I'd throw myself on my knees and give thanks to the gods who live in buffalo skulls. I'd pray no more virgins be thrown into the bogs, no more lotus flowers be eaten by the innocent, but I don't believe in praying."

"You don't have to pray," X said. "You can just write a policy requiring that employees get bathroom breaks, and that management stop drugging workers with toxic fumes."

C squinted her eyes the way she had that first night when she told him the big white penis jokes. "The key to my success is to know what I know *and what I don't know*."

She put her elbows on the table and leaned across her plate. "And one thing I don't know anything about is —" and here she pronounced the words as if she couldn't imagine anything more boring, "is *running a shoestring factory!*"

"But you own it!" X said.

"I own a lot of companies," she said, and laughed. "Me and thousands of other stockholders!" Then she leaned even farther across the table and kissed X on the forehead, leaving a wet spot that he resisted wiping. He looked away from his food and blinked. The sun cast such a clear light on the distant hills that it threatened to break his heart.

Suddenly he had an idea. "I have one request."

63

"Anything," she said.

"I'd like to have a mural painted on the wall surrounding the Great Lawn of the Management Suite Campus."

"That big wall?" C leaned back and lifted her napkin off her lap, lay it across her plate. She was finished. "I suppose it needs to be painted anyway."

The pollster, the muralist, and the danger of realism

X's only office responsibility was to put C's money in envelopes, write the sum on the outside, and stack the envelopes. He was allowed to take some of the money if he liked, but not too much. He had a phone, but the only two calls he got in the first six months were from a prankster and a sexy female pollster, whose semifamiliar voice coaxed answers from him like ejaculations.

"You let people take advantage of you. True or false."

"True."

"Lately, you often feel like smashing things."

X held the receiver in his hand like a club, squeezed it, contemplated the possibilities. "True."

"You try to please others even when you don't like them."

"True." He wanted to please the pollster.

"You dislike me."

"True." He felt an intense hatred for her that very moment that he could neither explain nor wish away.

"You enjoy suffering."

He thought of his work in the shoelace factory, which made him suddenly very lonely. A vacuum inside took his stomach away and he felt ashamed and covered his face, bowed his head.

"False," he said.

"Lately you feel like crying without any reason."

Could she see him? Was that ridicule he heard in her voice?

"Would you like me to repeat the question?"

"No," he said. He wiped his eyes. But he wasn't crying for no reason. He had plenty to cry about. Didn't everybody? "False," he said finally.

"You are a very erratic person, changing your mind and feelings all the time."

Outside his window, the western sky was a magnificent scarlet. The world was undeniably full of promise, wasn't it? There was always something else around the corner, and wasn't he a free man in a free country with a great economic system?

"True," he said.

The pollster thanked him and hung up, which is when X realized how he knew her voice. It was the woman in pink lamé. Or somebody with a similar voice. He tried to trace the call but couldn't. He drummed his fingers on the desk and bit his lower lip. He wondered if she'd call again. He'd often wondered what had become of her since she'd been dragged off screaming into that horrible night, and was glad to believe she was alive and working for a polling company. He sighed with joy and relief, opened another envelope, counted the money, slipped a couple of bills into his pocket, and replaced the money in the envelope and wrote the sum total on the envelope in pencil.

He ate lunch that day with the malformed boy, who'd been put in charge of handicapped employment and access for people with disabilities. The boy was no longer allowed to beat people and was dying of boredom.

"Didn't you tell me once you were an artist?" X asked.

The boy didn't remember ever saying such a thing, but he nodded anyway.

"Well, I need somebody to paint a mural on that long wall across the Great Lawn."

"A mural of what?"

"Of the shoelace factory," X said. "All of these people here are supported by that factory, and they don't even know what it looks like."

The malformed boy brightened at the idea. He began work immediately, and in six months had painted *A View from the Catwalk,* which captured the magnificent colors, the feel of abundant productivity, and the vast genius of material creation. The mural was extremely popular. People came from all over the world to see it. They praised its technical merits, of which there were many. And they praised C and X because they'd hired a painter with physical handicaps, and they praised the malformed boy for his talent. His success became an industry of its own. Entire departments were formed at art schools to study the neglected work of malformed painters, and as a visiting artist, the boy gave lectures on how he was able to get rich and famous despite having been shot in the head and thrown out of a moving car. Soon he left C's employment to paint similar murals at other corporate headquarters around the globe.

X stayed on. He tried to be satisfied with his job, but he wasn't. He tried to feel satisfied with the mural, too, but couldn't. There was something missing. It had captured the beauty of the factory, but none of the humanity. None of the suffering. The workers were noble stick figures, tiny, a decorative detail in the vast sweep of the scene. C traveled a lot, and when she was gone and he was unable to have diverting sexual relations with her, X's life quickly grew flat. He filled his spare time by writing electronic memos to fellow employees involved in home improvement projects. He solved practical problems concerning footings and dry rot, and published weekly newsletters on topics such as the advantages and disadvantages of radiant floor heating versus forced air. He walked the carpeted tunnel every day to Corpus Health, where he shot hoops, played handball, or climbed the Stairmaster. But as much as exercise helped him relieve stress, he could never get one thing off his mind. Each day, before passing into the club, he had to stop at the laundry window, where a young girl handed him his clean towel and gym clothes in a bag. He tried to divert his eyes, but couldn't help looking at her face, which seemed to him identical to the face of the Ethiopian girl who had died next to him at the shoestring factory. And even more bizarre, the old man working the washers behind her had the same vaguely Asian features as the dead old man.

One day he couldn't help but ask them if they'd ever worked in the shoestring factory. They both looked at him blankly, without speaking. He repeated the question, and when again they didn't speak, he realized they couldn't understand a word he said.

Late one night, when C was out of town traveling somewhere, X left their luxury condo apartment, drove to the corporate campus, and let himself in. He'd brought a paintbrush and paint, and he walked along the mural until he'd located the vat where he used to work. He looked at the squiggly little lines that the malformed boy had painted to represent the workers. He dipped his paintbrush into the paint, and he painted a face on one of the lines: the face of the Ethiopian girl. He painted it so small that the only way he could see it was under a magnifying glass. Satisfied that he'd captured her expression, he painted the old man's face on another squiggly line. Then he washed the brush and he left.

His work was so skillful that nobody noticed that the mural (the work of art, *the masterpiece,* as people had taken to calling it) had been changed. Nobody said, "Hey, who are those dead people on the factory floor?"

But nevertheless, people who looked at the mural reacted differently. Both visitors and employees seemed to gaze at it longer, more deeply, and instead of turning away from it with a self-satisfied, pleased expression, saying, Wow, that's amazing! they turned away troubled, and often didn't speak, couldn't speak, because the mural had touched them in an unexplainable way.

The result was disastrous. The optimistic and self-congratulatory attitude among headquarter employees had been slightly but undeniably altered. People were less certain in their notion that the company was Good, and that they were living their lives in a Good way. A few top management people quietly resigned their positions to join the Peace Corps, or made other equally backward or anachronistic life changes. A trickle of employees began to sell their stock, which quickly snowballed into a general malaise of investor confidence. The value of the stock dipped, which fueled more sales, causing the price to drop even lower.

Profits also sagged, because expenses had risen astronomically. The company had begun to receive, and to pay, huge bills for "strategic services." Instead of opening envelopes fat with cash, X sat at his desk opening envelopes with only a few coins.

"It doesn't matter," C said to him on the phone one evening from a distant hotel room when he described the company's desperate fix. "I don't need it anyway."

X thought of the Ethiopian towel girl, and the vaguely Asian laundry man. "But others do," he said.

C laughed uproariously. "What can I do?" she said. "I'm one woman, with two relatively well-formed but small breasts, and you want me to feed the world?"

One of the last times X walked down the hallway to Corpus Health, an emergency phone rang. He answered it and recognized immediately the voice of the woman in pink lamé. "Sir, I'm taking a survey, if you would be so kind."

"What kind of survey?"

"It's about chronic pain and disillusionment."

X's stomach turned with nervous glee. He was happy to hear this voice. He thought of their days together in the market, those wild successful days.

"Of course," he said.

"Keep in mind, sir, that we are scientists doing measurements, nothing more. Precision and accuracy are what we are looking for in your answers. Is that clear?"

"Yes," he said.

"Okay," she said. "There is substantial evidence linking feelings of sexual inadequacy on the part of cavalry officers with some of the biggest Indian massacres. True or false."

He didn't understand the question. He said, "What?"

"Speech impediments. Chemical dependencies. Co-dependencies, racial hatreds, un-counseled grief, hazardous wagon travel, and vaginal dryness are some of the undiagnosed disabilities of eighteenth- and nineteenth-century European colonizers."

X was speechless.

"Sir?"

"I don't know."

"And one more?"

"Go ahead."

"Can a child who is raised in a closet imagine God?"

X hesitated. "May I pass on this one?"

"Of course," she said. "In fact, I think I . . ." Her voice faded. "I think I need . . ."

X was terrified she was going to hang up. He said, "You

need to be certain. You need to know how it will end. You need cause and effect to be clear. And you would like very much to find a man you care for deeply."

Dead silence on the other end. X waited, picturing her sweet doughy face moving back and forth involuntarily.

"Sir?" came the voice, finally. "Are you who I think you are?"

"Are you?"

"I'm giving the survey," she said.

"Okay. Repeat the question."

"You are who I think you are. True or false."

X waited as long as he could, leaning against the carpeted wall of the tunnel, looking up through a tube in the ceiling to a perfect circle of blue sky. He imagined the sky spreading out forever past gleaming buildings and bushes trimmed like gargoyles, past the sweet cloud of descended despair. In his mind he flew like a bird over a vast and fertile land growing barley, malt, hops, and wheat. On his tongue was a line of poetry that he remembered learning years ago, but before he could say the words it was gone.

"I am," he said, and heard her sigh.

X and the woman in pink lamé go to sea, which they quickly learn is no place for a woman in pink lamé

X sat watching TV in C's condo when the woman in pink lamé knocked on the door. He opened it and she came in. Her dress was a little worse for the wear, but her pink makeup had been freshly applied. They embraced, and X took her sweet, moving head between his hands and kissed her salty, teary cheeks.

"Tell me what happened since that awful night," X said.

So she told him how she'd been taken away by a band of drug smugglers who lived in the hills, and how she had to join them or be staked to the earth for the ants to devour. It was hard at first, but it wasn't too long before she'd established a romantic relationship with the head smuggler, a ruthless ex-corporate raider everybody called Fungo. For a few years she believed she must have died and gone to heaven, hiking in the great outdoors every day, moving product that required no marketing campaign to bolster demand, sleeping between thick bearskins with Fungo, who surprisingly was quite an idealist, believing fervently in Global Free Trade, and resisting government regulation with his every waking breath.

Here the woman in pink lamé paused, and her lower lip protruded in sadness. "Unfortunately, Fungo dropped dead at my feet one morning. Brain aneurysm, I believe, but everybody else thought I killed him to get control of his sales organization. I barely escaped with my life, making my way north to the border and finding work with The Answer Company doing telephone surveys on politics, clothing, sports, food, and sex."

"Sex?"

"We asked people to describe their sexual activities," she said. "Then we checked them out with actual satellite photos."

"Did they lie?" X said.

She smiled and raised her penciled eyebrows playfully. "Lie and lay, lay and lie — Who can tell them apart anymore? Now tell me about you."

X did, and before he finished telling about the factory she was crying again, and kissing his hands, which still had a bit of dye staining the creases. Unfortunately, it was while she was on her knees in front of X, her lips on his fingers, that C arrived home from her business trip. She stood in the doorway with her bags, watching.

X tried to tell her that the woman in pink lamé was his old friend and business partner, and they'd had a platonic relationship, but C put her hands over her ears and closed her eyes and screamed, "DON'T YOU LIE TO ME IN MY OWN HOME!"

The bodyguard with whom C always traveled grabbed the woman in pink lamé by the back of the neck, lifted her like a kitten, and put her outside the apartment door. Then he tried to do the same to X, but X reached for a kitchen knife and plunged it into the bodyguard's chest, crumpling him. He'd never stabbed anyone before and was surprised at how easy it was.

Then he chose to leave C screaming, her eyes closed and her hands still covering her ears, and he joined the mobile woman in pink lamé outside.

They followed the coastal highway and spent the first evening sleeping in the grass on the side of the road, the second in a ditch at the border, and the third in a dive hotel in a grimy foreign port. The woman in pink lamé looked for work in sales and X for a job in the building field, but the local prospects were dreary to none. The majority of the retail work was done by little girls balancing buckets full of lemons, spicy meat, jawbreakers, earrings, watches, hammocks, or hot, steamy tortillas on their heads. And the only homes being built were pieced together with wooden pallets, plastic sheeting, and scraps of corrugated zinc.

After a hungry couple of days and nights, X and the woman in pink lamé secured positions as auxiliary crew on an ocean freighter carrying bazookas, computer chips, and mangos. Also computer screens and heroin stuffed into the computer screens. Also, in sealed containers, three hundred smuggled workers making a brave choice for mobility.

X and the woman in pink lamé felt fortunate and grateful to get the jobs. They were assigned an above-deck cabin, and the woman in pink lamé praised the accommodations, but that evening, soon after the ship hit the high seas, the other sailors tied up X and took the woman in pink lamé into another room. They formed an orderly line down the hallway so they could take turns having their way with her. X heard her screams for a while, but then he didn't hear anything. He could hear the sailors laughing, and saw one of them wearing only her black pumps, and another, a short one with a pock-scarred face, running up and down the hallway wearing the pink lamé dress.

"Hey!" X said.

But they ignored him.

In the morning he woke to find the woman in pink lamé, wearing her shoes and dress again, squatting beside him to untie his hands. She tried to smile, but something significant was different. That's when X noticed that her head was no longer moving. She looked at him with her face terrifyingly still and a great dark space behind her eyes, as if something living had been pumped out of her by all of those sailors. When his hands were free, he reached to touch her but she pulled away as though his hands were hot.

"I'll be all right," she said.

X stood. By the pitch and roll of the ship, he knew the seas were up. "Are you hungry?"

"No," she said.

In the cafeteria at breakfast he sat alone but could feel the crewmen watch him as he ate. Or tried to eat. The motion of the ship was making him sick, and the eyes of the crewmen filled him with hate. Finally, the short one with the pocked face cornered him.

"The guys asked me to tell you we're all real sorry about last night," he said.

X looked up from his oatmeal, and all of the young men's faces looked sad and long and sorry.

"Heck," said the pocked one. "We were all drunked up. You know how that goes."

X still didn't speak. He wasn't eating anymore.

"Most of us have anger issues," said one with a watch cap. "Our mothers were cruel, and our lovers either stingy or mercenary."

"We need counseling," interrupted a sailor who hadn't spoken before. "We admit it. We need to talk to a professional just as badly as we need pussy."

X kept remembering the vacant look in his friend's eyes, and he couldn't stand hearing the talk anymore, or seeing the faces. So he got up to fill a bag with bread and fruit to take back to the cabin so he and the woman in pink lamé wouldn't have to see any of these men again. He also poured a cup of coffee. With his hands full, he headed for the door. Ten steps away, eight, six, four. Then something made him stop and turn back to the men. Some remnant of hope.

"Just try to imagine a world without violence toward women," he said, his voice faltering.

Silence. The sailors blinked stupidly at one another, then looked to the floor. Were they trying to imagine it? The bud of hope blossomed in X, but Watch Cap looked up, his smile quickly malevolent.

"What about violence toward men? Is that allowed?"

Before X could answer, he heard a scream of laughter. Chairs suddenly slid across the floor as the crewmen leaped to their feet. X was thrown on the floor and pummeled and kicked and pummeled and kicked some more. He wanted to lose consciousness but didn't. He felt every blow, every chipped tooth and cracked rib, every broken blood vessel. For many terrible moments he lay hoping he'd die but then he remembered the woman in pink lamé sleeping in their room, and he knew he had to live. So he did. It was a matter of choice. And when the beating was over and the sailors dispersed to their daily work, he crawled to the cabin with as much food as his hands could slide along the deck in front of him.

They slipped off the boat in a gray city whose markets had recently opened after decades of corrupt government control. Mufflerless buses and cars and motorcycles wove madly along potholed streets. Vacant lots were piled with toxic garbage and rusting steel from construction jobs half finished. On the crowded sidewalks, pioneer businessmen wore telephone headsets and spoke an assortment of languages to associates, clients, and family. "Fredrickson's transferred, and the whole company's gone apeshit!" said a man passing close by. "If it'd make you more comfortable," said a woman, "I could profile some of our value-enhancement demand initiatives!" "Say hi to Da-da!" a man shouted before stepping past X. *"Da-da woves wou!"*

The result was a terrible din, but apparently big money was being made, as many of these people wore very nice clothing, and some were shopping from open catalogs while they walked.

Hungry and broke, X and the woman in pink lamé needed work, which would be difficult to find in the shape they were in. X's head was swollen and purple, only one of his eyes opened, and only six teeth remained in his mouth. The woman in pink lamé was worse. Broken on the inside, she could barely get herself out of bed each morning. She'd sit and stare at whatever was in front of her, occasionally shouting strange things like, "That bunny's mine!"

X found them a room. She sat on the bed and he turned her slightly so she could at least look out the window at the sky, where chimney swifts flew, but she stood up and tried to open it, tried to get out.

He helped her back to the bed and turned her toward the wall and waited until he was satisfied she was not going to try to get out the window again. Then he left and wandered the streets until he was out of the neighborhood of well-dressed pioneers talking loudly on telephone headsets and into an older, quieter part of town. He stood alongside some railroad tracks watching shirtless, shoeless black men push flatcars. About twenty or thirty men pushed each car, and as they pushed they sang pre-market economy spirituals that raised the hair on the back of his neck.

X got into a line of job seekers that stretched along the tracks and disappeared into the side door of a warehouse. A woman dressed in red boots and black jodhpurs, a riding crop tucked under her arm, walked the length of the line.

"Keep to the right!" she shouted in a variety of languages. "Those to be interviewed, keep to the right!"

X squeezed to the right with everybody else. He wondered, Who was supposed to go to the left? The woman in front of him carried a fancy French telephone. She whispered to X that she'd come prepared for a phone call.

"I see that," X said.

As if to parody the capitalist pioneers in the other part of town, she repeatedly lifted the receiver to her ear, shouted something unintelligible, and then slammed it down again. She was making X nervous. He didn't know what the job was, but he could feel in his stomach and his bones how much he needed it — so he didn't like this woman with the telephone because she wanted the job as much as he did! Why hadn't he brought *his* telephone?

He didn't have time to ponder this question for long because suddenly he was inside the warehouse, moving up the stairs and into a large hall with the rest of the applicants, past the boss woman with red boots and black jodhpurs. She smiled with her lips only while inspecting each candidate.

X sat down at the end of a long line of chairs that snaked around the edge of a gymnasium. He sat next to a man who carried a glass terrarium that held a pile of sand with holes in it. The man had a very earnest face, and he gestured sharply with his hands, every now and then tapping the glass with his finger.

"I'm trained in species recovery," he said, his accent thick. "There's a colony of triceratops in here."

X was skeptical, but he tried not to be. "When do they come out?"

"I don't know," the man said. "I've never seen them."

"Never?"

"Only their sign."

"What's that look like."

The man laughed as though X were an idiot. "Dinosaur shit. What else?"

X continued studying the terrarium for any sign of life. All he saw was some sand with a couple of holes big enough for mice. There was no plant life, no tracks, no water, no shit.

"Why don't you just reach in there and push the dirt away?"

The man was flabbergasted, his face red. "Why don't I push the dirt away?"

X nodded.

"Because they'd bite my fingers off! And I only have one left!" He held up both hands. Sure enough, all of his fingers were gone at the joint connecting them to the hand. The finger he'd been tapping the glass with was the only finger he had left. X suddenly felt great sympathy for this odd, fingerless man.

Nearby, a tall, thin woman wearing a biplane pilot outfit spread her arms and mimicked the sound of an airplane. She did some swoops as though flying. A tall, thin man followed along at her side.

"What's her problem?" X asked the man with the triceratops.

"She's deaf. She deafened herself as a sacrifice."

"To what?" X asked.

"For the job."

Suddenly X felt stupid. He understood then that all of

the other applicants had come bearing a gift or a sacrifice. Obviously the guy with one finger had done both.

"What's your sacrifice?" X asked the deaf woman's friend, the man tilting his head like a dog.

"Two things, actually," the man said. "For one, I've had a good chunk of my duodenum lopped off and sent in under glass. So they should have received that already. But the main thing is that I'm with her, the airplane woman. That enough?"

Desperate for a distraction, X turned his attention to the quiet older man sitting behind him. The man was bald and had a flat nose that looked as though it had been broken repeatedly. He wore blue jeans and a red flannel shirt rolled up to his elbows, exposing thick, hairy forearms. On his lap he held a large blue book.

"Good book?" X asked.

The man held it up. On the cover was printed JOE'S BOOK in large black letters. X looked at the man, who smiled, showing lots of small, yellow teeth.

"Are you the author?" X said.

Joe grinned with pride and folded his arms in front of his chest. "I write a few stories at chow every day. Want me to read one out loud?"

X rested his tired, wounded, and distorted head in his hands. "Sure," he said. "It'll kill some time."

A short story of endurance and survival and a Dr. Fingerdoo protégé interview

"The fall I was sixteen," Joe began reading, "I worked as a woodcutter in a hunting camp, but for months I pestered my boss to let me pack and pull a string of mules. On the last day he finally said yes, so I mounted my horse, all set to pull eight mules packed with quartered elk thirty-two miles out of the wilderness by myself. I was so happy and dumb I could have croaked.

"After a few miles the trail began a series of switchbacks up a horseshoe canyon. The weather turned bad, and it began to snow. A rock face on one side and a five-hundred-foot drop on the other, the trail was so narrow that in order to keep from falling over the cliff the packed mules rubbed against the rock wall.

"Leading a string of pack animals in the snow is like dragging a chain, and you can feel when suddenly you're dragging only half. Close to the top, I knew something was wrong. I led the string to a place where the trail widened, then got off my horse and wormed my way back. I was missing three animals. I found two a short way down the trail, and I urged them up through shin-deep snow and tied them with the others. I was scared to death about the third mule, though. I knew I'd have to go back until I found it, so I took the packs off all the animals because I didn't know how long it was going to take to get back, and I didn't want them standing for hours with their packs on.

"It was almost dark by the time I worked my way down the switchbacks to a little meadow underneath the cliff, which is where I found the missing mule, belly deep in snow, the side packs spread like wings. Figuring I'd lead the old boy out, I took off his pack, which is when I saw his back was broke. That's when I started to cry. I was cold and in big trouble. The only thing I could think to do was kill the mule, put him out of his misery, but I'd left my rifle on top with the rest of the string, and all I had was a pocketknife. I reached around his head and started to cut, but he bellowed and threw his head this way and that, so I hung on and reached under his throat and sawed away. Sawing and bawling, and blood everywhere! You've never seen as much blood as comes out of a mule with its throat slit. Finally, when it was done, all I'm thinking is I've lost a mule and I can't lose the elk meat, too. So I struggled though the waist-deep snow with the pack and the elk quarter, my feet so cold they could barely feel the ground. I was thinking I didn't have the strength for this, but I worked my way up the trail anyway thinking this is how I'm going to die, goddamn it. Mule blood all over me, tears, a freezing hunk of elk in my hand.

"Somehow I kept moving. Partly from the fear of getting chewed out by my boss, and partly from shame whenever I remembered how I practically begged to pull the string by myself. It took me all night and then some to work my way those few miles up those snowy switchbacks, and I don't really remember much about it. I only remember my boss coming along about midmorning with the hunters. I was up top by then, trying to repack the string. He laid into me, just like I thought he would. Not for losing a mule, though. No, he was mad as a wet cat because I had gone back in that weather. Because I'd risked my life. Funny, because I was thinking that that was the one thing I did right. I only wanted to do the job well, or take the least loss when I did it poorly, and here's my boss telling me it wasn't worth the effort. To add to everything else, now I was confused. I remember all the hunters sitting way up high on their horses looking down at me as if I were some sort of bloody alien, which I can see now I clearly was.

"I don't remember much about the seven-hour ride out of there. I figure I was pretty much in shock from the cold."

When he finished reading, Joe closed the book and swallowed a lump. "That was the first time I almost died," he said. "And there's been quite a few times since, come to think about it."

X was so moved by the story he could have cried. The things people manage to live through! The hope, the idealism, the frozen tears!

"That's gross," said the airplane woman, who wasn't deaf after all. She removed her leather helmet and began to brush her auburn hair. "I don't relate well to blood."

She joined a number of listeners who'd pulled chairs into a circle to form an ad hoc marketing survey group.

"It doesn't give me that triumphant feeling I like in a survival story," said the woman with the French telephone.

"I enjoy a story with more of a love interest," said another. "Something funnier and not so outdoorsy."

"Personally," said the one-fingered man, his thick brow creased, "I can't make out just what exactly I'm supposed to bring to the text."

"Who cares?" X said from outside the circle. "It's a story about a kid trying to do something hard. Trying beyond his endurance to do a man's work well, and to survive."

"Man's work?" said the airplane woman. "That's sexist! And the dead mule/father motif trivializes and excludes women."

"Is the dead mule a *symbol* of something?"

"It's Southern Fiction," said a young man with pursed lips and studious glasses who seemed to be positioning himself as the discussion leader, "which *by definition* has dead mules in it."

Everybody in the marketing survey group nodded.

During X's interview, a handsome man wearing a telephone headset introduced himself as a protégé of the famous Dr. Fingerdoo.

"I'm honored," X said. "I'm looking for something in the building game."

The Fingerdoo protégé smiled condescendingly and sat

down. "In today's opening markets, we all need to have a little Proteus in us, don't we?"

X didn't know what Proteus was, but he smiled and nodded anyway.

"Are you any good with keys?" the protégé asked.

"Keys?"

"Yes."

"How do you mean, *good with keys*?"

The protégé wrote something on a clipboard. He sat with one great massive thigh crossed over the top of the other. He took a long, patient breath. "Give us your background in keys," he said. "Your skill level."

X wondered what job he was applying for. "I am very good with keys," he said. "I've been using them to start cars and open locked things since I was a boy."

The Fingerdoo protégé stroked his Fingerdoo-like beard and raised a caterpillar eyebrow. He jotted down some more notes on the clipboard. He gestured to the stack of boxes the other applicants had left.

"Did you bring anything?"

"A gift?"

"We're looking for evidence of sacrifice. We want to know you've suffered. We don't believe in giving jobs to people who don't appreciate them. We believe that if you've sacrificed for the job, you won't quit on us."

X thought for a moment. He remembered how C had said that people who praise sacrifice are almost always talking about the sacrifice of others.

"Actually," he said, "I brought my mule."

"Your mule?"

"I cut his throat and he is dead and too big to drag up the stairs so I left him on the sidewalk."

"A dead mule." The protégé pronounced the words slowly as he wrote them on the clipboard. "Very good. And did you love the mule?"

"Very much."

The protégé looked at him carefully, cleared his throat. "Anything else?"

X had a sense that the dead mule was probably adequate, but because he was hungry, and because the woman in pink lamé was hungry, and because the protégé was obviously wondering about his swollen and purple head, X added, "And a lobotomy, of course."

The protégé put his lips together and made a sound that indicated he was impressed. He jotted something down.

"And your name?"

"X."

"Could you spell that please?"

"X"

The Fingerdoo protégé smiled as though that were just the right answer.

New work in an old market niche

X was given a set of keys on a long chain and a young partner named O' o'o', who asked X to simply call him O. They climbed into a van.

"What are we supposed to do?" X asked.

O drove very fast. "Good honest work!" He laughed as he maneuvered the van through the city traffic. "Here, take a look at these."

O handed X a stack of magazines from the floor of the van. On the cover of the top magazine was a photo of a smiling, naked, brown-skinned person with blond hair, lovely breasts, and a big penis. The magazine was called *Multiracial She-Males*.

"Kinda makes you wonder what's what and what ain't, right?"

X nodded. Every time he thought the world couldn't get any stranger, it did. He felt a terrible weariness come over him as he settled back to page through the magazine at countless more happy mixed-race hermaphrodites.

The first place X and O stopped was an adult video parlor next door to the opera house. O wore sunglasses and directed X to a pair in the glove box. Also in the glove box was a small rubber statue of the Virgin Mary. X picked it up and held it in his hand.

"Turn it around," O said. "Look at her from behind."

X did. He couldn't believe the transformation. With a turn, the rubber-robed Virgin became a rubber penis.

"The search for salvation necessitates blasphemy," O said.

"Huh?"

"You'll see what I mean. C'mon." He parked the van and got out. X followed him into Video Palace. O walked through the well-lighted racks filled with more gadgetry then videos and then into a long, dimly lit hallway with doors on both sides.

"Out! Everybody out!" O shouted, and the doors opened and well-dressed men scurried past them like roaches. When it was quiet again O chuckled nervously and entered the first booth. The reek of semen and sweat, the dirty green walls, the little TV screen behind dirty glass, and the slot for the quarters all made X want to puke, but O said, "Hang on, brother. Watch what I do."

He inserted the key just below the slot and slid out a drawer filled with coins. He emptied the coins into a cloth bag with a drawstring, then replaced the drawer. X noticed the holes in the wall just big enough to look through, or to slip your penis through, and he thought about the amazing faith necessary to do that, and thinking about that made his stomach even heavier and his knees weak.

"Glory holes," O explained.

If it weren't for the thought of the woman in pink lamé, helpless and hungry in the hotel room, X would have quit right there. But he couldn't. He had nothing else. He had to stick with it until he had another prospect. He had to keep his eyes open until he could again choose to be mobile.

X and O emptied all of the drawers in all of the booths, and by the time they finished, a fresh line of well-groomed consumers stood politely waiting to spend more discretionary coins. Many wore telephone headsets and conversed while they waited. One said, "We provide win-win scenarios and customer-focused solutions!" Another said, "We don't sell; we partner!"

Back in the van, O reached across the front seat to crank open X's window. "Hang in there, bub." He pulled out into traffic. They were driving down a broad avenue toward gleaming skyscrapers, but the sidewalks were jammed with shuffling, phoneless job seekers. Men, women, and children carried their pitiful personal offerings in cages and boxes and bags.

"Give me your maxed-out, your low-income, your recently relocated, yearning to . . ."

"What?"

"I can't help it," O said, grinning. "It just makes me feel better to know that if the riffraff could get away with it," he gestured toward the crowd on the sidewalk, "they'd kill to be where we are right now."

Natural disaster, a new job, and again X finds himself in a different country entirely

When X got back from work that evening, he carried a bag of sweet rolls for the woman in pink lamé to nibble on before bed. But she was gone, and the window to their tiny room stood open. He looked out at the busy street, two stories below, and saw no sign that she had jumped. Could she have flown? Anything was possible, X was beginning to understand, but she really didn't have the build for flying.

Hours later, after having searched the neighborhood alleys and bars, X returned lonely and sad to his room. He lay on the bed and thought about his life long ago in a temperate land of pretty hills and thick soil, where people lived in sturdy, well-built homes and earned sufficient pay and leisure time for an occasional trip to the tropics. His youth in Wonderland had been a marvelous dream in which true hardship and suffering were distant enough to explain away as things that happen to people who "just don't get it," or to people whose societies have not "developed" sufficiently. And so his own prosperity made perfect sense: He'd studied and earned degrees, and he learned what he knew about building techniques and materials by working hard. He had shared this knowledge with others, and it made a difference in their lives, a difference they were willing to pay for. He knew the same things now and yet earned his money emptying coin boxes in porno shops.

Could C have been right when she said there was no reasonable connection between virtue and well-being? Didn't many kind, good, and talented people suffer, while many cruel and stupid people thrive? Despite what Dr. Fingerdoo and his protégés proclaimed, the Global Free Market could not be trusted to make the world a better place. It gave and took arbitrarily or mysteriously. Which perhaps is why people worshiped it so.

X lay in bed and stared at the dark ceiling of his room that reflected stripes of yellow light from the window. If he'd been born a druid, he'd have trusted in his bones that the spirits determining his fate lived in the trunks of trees. But he'd been born at a later time, and he trusted in other things. Had he been conned about the nature and source of Providence and Justice? And by whom?

But philosophical questions mattered less to him than personal questions, such as Where was the woman in pink lamé? And would he ever see C again?

He rolled over onto his stomach, and to make himself feel better he thought about C's lovely round bottom and milk-chocolate skin, and he thought of the spicy smell of her cigarettes and despite the circumstances of their parting, he suddenly knew one thing for sure: He knew he'd never be happy without her.

Then, through the floor, X heard a rumbling, and the rumbling grew to a growling, and the growling to a shaking, and soon his bed felt like a ship on the ocean, rocking and rolling, sliding from one wall to the other. The noise was deafening now, like a train in the next room, and when the bed slid next to the window, X managed to grab the sill and peek out. The solid street was moving in waves like the surface of the sea! Terrified, he hung on until the wall split and the floor dropped, and then he was falling and then he wasn't.

Silence. He'd landed, miraculously, on his bed, the rubble of the hotel all around him. Fires had sprung up, and he made his way out into the smoky street. He walked around piles of rubble, around injured people screaming. A man ran down the street carrying a television under his arm like a football. Around the corner, more people ran by carrying power tools and armfuls of clothing off store racks. He paused when he saw a woman pointing to a pile of rubble, under which she'd apparently seen a child trapped. X dug quickly through the ruins of the house, tossing splintered studs this way and that, pushing ceiling and floor joists, and finally he pulled the thin boy out.

By the time he did, however, the woman behind him had disappeared into the gloom.

Tears streaking the ragged boy's soot-caked cheeks, he asked, "Where are you going?"

X shrugged.

"Take me with you!"

X started walking. He didn't know where he was going

95

but he was moving quickly through the broken city, the boy behind him. Soon another waif had joined them. Then another and another. X stepped around burning and smashed cars, shattered glass, bits of crumpled towers, toppled trees. The crowd of boys behind him grew. In his head was the view from his deck in Wonderland on an August morning, the green hollow filled with a low fog, the yellow sun shining through in spots and making the dew sparkle.

Then he turned a blind corner and bumped into a soldier decked out in green fatigues, goggles, and a gas mask. From the soldier's belt hung a dazzling array of high-tech devices, and in his hand was a magic sword.

"Excuse me," X said, and tried to step past him, but there were hundreds more soldiers in rank filling the street.

"Where are you going?" the soldier asked in a Wonderlandian accent.

"Someplace fair," X said. "Someplace good. Someplace where the market provides adequately for all citizens and solid rock doesn't jiggle like jelly."

The soldier lifted his magic sword and pressed it against X's neck. "Looks like we got a smart ass," he said over his shoulder.

"I just need a job," X said.

X was taken to a brand-new Wonderlandian army base, given a uniform, and over the next several weeks trained with other new recruits to use high-tech gadgetry and magic swords. One morning they were filed into a jet plane with no windows and flown for hours and hours to a remote corner of the planet. When they were herded out of the plane it was still morning, and the air smelled damp and rotten. They were told to stand on the oven-hot tarmac and wait, and because they were so well trained, they did just that. All day and through the night, and finally in the morning they were marched into a dark briefing room, where a general displayed a series of PowerPoint maps and diagrams.

When the lights finally came up, he said, "We Wonderlandians are not a warlike people. We are a good people. So we wouldn't be doing this without a good reason."

The heads of hundreds of exhausted soldiers nodded. Beneath his heavy helmet, X nodded too.

"In this jungle land," the general said, "the indigenous population has remained ignorant, religious fanatics who claim the forest is full of fairies that get offended at a little oil drilling."

The same hundreds of heads that a moment ago nodded now shook slowly from side to side, amazed.

"Imagine," the general said, "a land with no economy to speak of!"

A collective gasp rose from the mass of exhausted soldiers.

The general paused and cleared his throat. "Many people here have been without jobs their entire lives!"

An immense sigh of incredulity. Even X found himself amazed that in this day and age people lived without jobs.

"Unemployed!" the general said, pounding the podium as if there was just no darn reason for such sadness. "As were their parents and grandparents! Which is one of the reasons that they seem to have enough leisure time to go around blowing up pipelines and oil derricks, and terrorizing decent businessmen who have come here offering jobs."

"How will we know them when we see them?" a soldier shouted from the crowd.

The general flicked another switch and giant photos of the enemy came up on the screen behind him. He used the electronic arrow to point. "The men wear long yellow gourds over their dongs," he said. "And the women paint their titties with ochre."

The next morning X marched with the rest of the troops through the jungle and into the surrounding hills, where they rounded up representatives of the indigenous population, tied their hands, and marched them in a line through a valley blackened by napalm. In every village they came to more gourd-covered or ochre-painted people were persuaded at gunpoint to join the march. They waded through silted rivers smelling of crude oil, over recently cut jungle now growing grass to feed cows to feed pipeline workers. Some of the prisoners in the column fell over dead, but the majority kept marching. The soldier next to X was a talker who said he missed his girl back home. He said he missed her so much he thought he might die of missing her.

A melancholy pause followed. Sweat dripped down X's face. His legs hurt, and his shoulders hurt from his pack, and his arms hurt from carrying the heavy magic sword.

The talker wondered aloud if his girl missed him as much as he missed her, and then worked his way around to the conclusion that he didn't believe she could, because he didn't see how anybody could feel what he felt and stay alive long.

"I love her so much," the talker said. "I hope she's been true."

Another pause, during which X considered and then rejected the notion of reassuring the talker that indeed his gal had been true.

"She likes sex *a lot*!" the soldier said. "And I don't see how anybody who likes something as much as she likes that can resist for long, especially as she's pretty enough to have offers."

They marched and marched. X was tired of walking, and tired of the heat, and so tired of listening to the talker talk that he wanted to scream. Occasionally a prisoner stumbled on the trail ahead of him, and X hurried to offer a helping hand before one of the more ambitious boy soldiers arrived to beat the fallen prisoner.

The talker continued talking through it all: "If I ever get out of this jungle alive, and if she's been true, I'll marry her. I love her so much. But if she hasn't been true, I . . ."

That's when they were ambushed by guerrillas hiding in the trees, and the soldier next to X, the talker, fell over in midsentence, his face in agony as blood geysered from a wound in his throat. X tried to put his hand over the hole, but the blood squirted between his fingers, and he watched the talker's face grow pale as the words coming out of his mouth turned to a gurgle, and then to silence.

The enemy fire grew even more intense. X kept his head down, so he couldn't even see where it was coming from, and he felt warm urine soak his pants. The guerrillas lobbed primitive, low-tech mortars that occasionally scored direct hits and sent body parts hurling into the air. Prisoners ran every which way, scattering into the forest. X could hear wounded soldiers screaming for help, waving their magic swords impotently in the air. Then he heard his commander call for air support, and within minutes the planes arrived, and they flattened the surrounding jungle with a deafening fireball. The shooting stopped. X stood up with the rest of the soldiers who weren't wounded. On the way out, they stepped over hundreds of burned enemy bodies. The smell was almost unbearable. One of the boy soldiers said, "I guess we kicked their asses!"

Before they got to the base, X veered off into the forest as though to shit, but chose to keep going. Mobility and Choice. He didn't know where he was going, only that he'd dropped his magic sword some time ago and was still going.

He crossed the high mountains on foot and came down a long winding trail into a valley full of primary colors. Terraces of abundant organic food crops were separated by serpentine stone walls draped with hanging flowers. The half-naked indigenous people he met on the trail hadn't heard about the war on the other side of the mountain, so despite his army uniform, they were unafraid. When they saw him, they smiled and waved, and called out to him a three-word phrase in their gentle-sounding language. The three words meant Ugly Yellow Dog! which was the indigenous people's expression for *stranger*, but X naturally assumed they were greeting him, and he waved and said "Hello!"

By the time he arrived in a village, he was tired and hungry. He looked around for a commercial place to buy something to eat but found none. The stick-and-grass homes were neat, the gardens lovely, but there was something odd painted on the front door of every hut: a colorful six-foot-tall penis.

He stepped up to one of the huts to inquire about a room, knocked on a large purple glans spouting silver semen, and a smiling man wearing nothing but a loincloth answered the door. Behind him stood three similarly dressed young women. Invited in, X was offered a chair and plates of fruits and meats. When he had eaten his fill, he was given a warm bath by two of the women, dried gently with a lavender towel, and escorted to bed, where he was gratified sexually, and then left to sleep soundly and happily. In the morning he was wakened by two more playful women, neighbors, apparently, who held him down and enthusiastically took from him their pleasure.

When they finished, he was given breakfast and a comfortable chair to sit on outside the house. The sky was blue, and while a line of women swept the clay street clean, children laughed and played at their feet. Sometime in the middle of the day he was fed again, and neighbor men came and said, "Ugly Yellow Dog!" then laughed and sat with him to smoke. The day passed that way, and in the evening more eager women came to tuck him in. In the dark before he drifted off, he lay in his bed and listened through the grass wall to the sounds of the village night: crickets, an owl, and an occasional female orgasmic sigh from one of the surrounding huts.

Days passed, then weeks. X had never been in a happier place. Wagonloads of food came in from the country daily, and craftsmen worked a few hours in the morning to keep the town supplied with the basic items people needed to cook and sit and sleep. The huts were made of sticks and straw, and the corners were not square, and light showed through cracks in the wall, but the roofs were watertight and nobody seemed to worry, or think about adding a deck, or refurbishing the kitchen with a stone-countered island, or adding a spare room, new windows or skylight. Goods were exchanged without money, and in fact the only use X noticed for paper money was as something pretty to hang in homes. Piece by piece, he gave away his soldier uniform — the helmet, the boots, the socks, the shirt — and soon all he wore were pants, which he'd cut off so he looked more like the other men.

One day children came up to him and excitedly yelled "Ugly Yellow Dog!" and pointed to X, and then pointed down toward the river. They took X's hand and pulled him along. Soon other people joined them, first pointing to X and then to the river. Curious, X let himself be led down to where he saw the malformed boy with his paints out, preparing to paint a penis on the front door of a new hut at the edge of town.

"It's you!" X said, happy to see him.

The boy snarled, even as X lifted the boy's malformed little body and did a dance to the delight of the crowd.

"So this is your work?" X asked, putting him down again.

The boy, no longer a boy, but a malformed man with a wrinkled face, nodded. He had his Cleveland Indians cap pulled down low to cover his bullet-hole scar. X noticed his broken and bent pretzel body stiff, no longer limber. "It was their custom before I got here. It's a protection against the spirits of impotence, of course. But I've pushed the form subtly, and I've become quite popular. I couldn't stand doing murals for corporations anymore."

The malformed boy turned and pointed to certain delicate touches he'd invented recently. "These are more what I'm feeling, you know," he said. "More who I am."

Only then did X notice the malformed boy was surrounded by groupies, both indigenous people and Ugly Yellow Dogs! who nodded at everything he said.

"You can't surpass this place for the artistic and copulatory opportunities," the malformed boy explained. "And because there aren't any good-paying jobs, few new people relocate here."

The groupies nodded in agreement. "But everybody shares," one of them said. "And the food's organic," said another. A young blonde woman with dreadlocks surrounding a very sweet face said, "Yeah, and people aren't so uptight about cocks and stuff!"

———

X stayed in the village for years. He lost track of time. The malformed boy came and went with his entourage, because his work required travel from village to village, decorating new doors, touching up faded paintings. X helped out building new huts in his village. He gathered sticks for the walls and bunched dry grass for the thatch. He worked a little in the terraced gardens, picked berries, and the days slipped away like wild horses over the hills.

But something in this paradise nagged him. At first he couldn't identify the source of his dissatisfaction. Then one day he knew. X missed friends and conversation. He missed being respected for something he knew. Here, despite their gentle hospitality, nobody cared what he said or tried to say. Their reaction when he spoke their language was to giggle, shake their heads condescendingly, and say to one another, "Aren't Ugly Yellow Dogs cute?"

And another thing was causing him unhappiness: despite the abundance of sexual pleasure, X missed C. Her smell, her wild grin, her shapely bottom and neck that he'd long ago sunk his badger teeth into. And he missed her words, too. Her goofy jokes and irreverent ideas. He wondered where she was, and how she was, and why she was so impossible to forget.

He also felt guilty whenever he thought about the woman in pink lamé. Guilty for not being able to protect her on the ship, guilty for leaving her alone in their room while he went to work. Where was she? And what other tortures might the world have invented for a soul as good and delicate as hers?

He announced he was leaving. The malformed boy, who happened to be passing through the village at the time, called him an idiot. X shrugged and conceded that might be true. But he was less happy than everybody else, and this difference was starting to make him miserable.

The malformed boy didn't understand. "You may be less happy than everybody else, but you are still happier than you would be on the other side, right?"

X shrugged. "Maybe," he said. "But the fact that people here are so happy has actually begun to make me *more* miserable. Like being with a woman who is moaning and cooing, and you're not feeling the same way. . . . Don't you begin to detest her?"

The malformed boy shook his head in disgust. "So what?" he said. "As a man, I'd be ashamed to let a little rancor get in the way of sex!"

The wandering search of pilgrim X, and how it ended

Remembering the words of his mother — "There's something new around every corner!" — X left the paradise valley on the vast continent across the globe from Wonderland. Pulled by the mysterious instinct of love, his pockets filled with paper money village people had used as wall decorations, he hiked over the high mountains and down into a foreign city where he went to an all-night restaurant and ordered a large plate of spicy noodles. He liked his sudden anonymity, and the sense of refuge offered by this clean, well-lighted place. A half dozen urchins, their faces shiny from sniffing glue, appeared outside the window and pointed to their open mouths. X ate until his belly was full, and then he scraped what he couldn't eat onto pieces of flatbread, and gave those to the hungry children.

As he walked down the grimy sidewalks searching for a cheap hotel, the dark of the city swallowed his feeling of well-being and replaced it with dread. X wondered what was wrong with him to have come back to a world in which children were abandoned to make bad choices on the street. He wondered if the purple-robed Dr. Fingerdoo might have been right when he long ago predicted that *Only after the Global Economy has expanded into all parts of the world, only after all peoples sacrifice their racist, superstitious, and nonmaterial indigenous cultures, only then will everybody's plates be heaped with noodles!*

X's head hurt and he couldn't think about it for long. Alone in his ancient hotel room that night, he found the comfort of sleep only by remembering C's joyful face when she'd leaned over him and told a string of obscene jokes on the first night they met.

The next morning he found an Internet café and did a thorough search for her. Nothing in world business, nothing in official government records. Nothing about the woman in pink lamé, either.

If they were alive, they couldn't be in Wonderland, where citizens and travelers left deep digital tracks. They must be a long way away, like him. But where?

In the years that followed, he traveled around a great deal, searching. Foreign retail hubs swept about him like dead leaves that were brightly colored but torn away from the branches. He would have stopped but found he was chasing two women, his memory of them often coming to him unaware, taking him altogether by surprise. Perhaps it was a familiar bit of music, or the sound of wild laughter. Perhaps he'd be walking along a street at night in some strange media market before he found a companion. He'd pass the lighted window of a shop where pink lamé was sold, or a pet store with baby badgers in the window, and then all at once he'd feel his friend or his lover touch his shoulder. He'd turn to look into her eyes and reach to embrace her. But she'd disappear into the empty air. *Oh woman in pink lamé! Oh C! Where have you gone?*

Quickly he'd cross the street, climb on a bus, hail a taxi to the next transportation hub. Choice and Mobility!

To support himself he took a series of jobs helping developing countries digitize their music, their stories, their art, their fetal tissue, their children's future, their memories, their sacred grounds, and even their food production so as to better market globally. It wasn't pleasant work, but it wasn't hard either. And in most countries his only other job choice was the sweatshop.

His idealism had been drummed out of him, but not his optimism. So onward he traveled, ever hopeful, through the land where people knelt at low tables and ate with sticks, through the land where people sat on mats and ate with their fingers, and back again into the land where people sat on chairs and ate with forks. When he couldn't find work, he took up juggling as a way to draw a crowd and earn a bowl of coins for his next meal.

One evening, while passing tired and hungry through a pious industrial city where the current style called for both men and women to wear masks and hooded capes in public, X paused on a busy street to set up his act. As soon as he'd removed his knives and torches from his bag, he noticed a crowd gathering across the street. Rather than try to compete for an audience, he repacked and approached. A woman stood on the hood of a car under a streetlight.

Her rubber mask formed grotesque and bloody features; her cape was a simple black. She paced back and forth on the car preaching chastity as a form of health care to a small crowd of malcontents. The crowd, most of them wearing animal masks, laughed and shouted words in a guttural language that denoted sexual acts, positions, body parts. The woman pointed to the sky, the color of dull yellow from reflected streetlamps, and said in the same guttural language, but with a Wonderlandian accent, "When the hoppers came they blackened our sky like a cloud, then descended and walked for three days, eating everything in sight, clogging creeks, forming their own dams and bridges, eating the paint on the barn, eating clothing left on the line, small children, and then suddenly all at once, as though a billion tiny synchronized watches had been passed out among the hoppers, they flew away!"

"So what's the point, sweetheart?" somebody yelled.

"The point is that we listen to the radio and watch videos, and we do that long enough, we just might forget that we are going to die."

"So what?"

"So chastity is a good and constant reminder. Desire has you by the short hairs. You're pinched between the fingers of biological longing and death."

At this she had to hesitate, pause, for the shrieking her comment produced in her audience of randy men.

"Tell us about it!"

"How does it feel, baby?"

The woman looked over the crowd through the slits in

her mask, waiting for quiet and a chance to continue. Finally, she said in a breathy whisper: "I feel a screaming in every cell of my body."

She shuddered there on the car hood. The crowd of watchers grew silent as she stood, arms at her side, face toward the sky, quivering.

"She's getting off," some guy said.

Another said, "Is she going to show us her butt?"

By now X was beginning to suspect something. The suspicion made him afraid because of the disappointment he'd feel if he were wrong. But even under the loose black cape he'd seen hints of the lovely round bottom he knew so well. . . . And the woman's voice, too, even speaking this foreign tongue, seemed familiar.

The preacher woman pointed down at X from the hood of the car. He self-consciously adjusted his own small turtle mask. "I can see he suffers pain," she said. "I can see he is a sinner. I believe I can help him!"

"Hang on to your wallet, boy," one of the men said, slapping X's back.

"Do you desire to know things?" she asked. "Is redemption a myth? Are we just trying to climb out of the slime? Are we contemptuous of beauty because it mocks our endeavors? Do you want a whiff of my flower?"

Yes, X admitted, without speaking. He wanted to kiss her feet, lick between her toes, up her calves, the backs of her knees. . . . Stop. What if he were wrong? What if she wasn't who he thought she was?

With all of his willpower he turned his attention from

the woman. Nearby, a man with a wooden warrior mask paced back and forth.

"Nice mask," X said.

The man raised his hand to touch it but stopped short. "I took an Authentic Action Adventure to a jungle island," he said from behind the mask. "We lived with natives for just under two weeks. It was an immersion thing. Really showed the culture, know what I mean?"

"They sold you the mask?"

"Hell no. I got it at the airport. We weren't allowed to buy anything artsy-craftsy from the natives."

"Weren't *allowed*?"

"Except for wild man juice. All you could drink!" He let out a yee-haa type scream that raised the hair on the back of X's neck and attracted the attention of the preacher woman.

"What are you two talking about?" she asked, still up on the hood of the car.

"His Authentic Action Adventure," X said, using all of his willpower to pretend he didn't suspect he knew her.

"Is that right?" She removed her left shoe and peeled a photograph from the instep. "I've been on one of those, too!"

X and the Wooden Warrior looked at the photo. It was a wallet-sized photo that showed C's beautiful face and wild red hair next to a black man with a painted white nose and a bone necklace. The man wore a feather-and-quill headdress that extended up and out, beyond the limits of the picture.

X handed the photo back to her, joy and jealousy dancing madly in his chest. He'd had some mighty fine erotic experiences of his own with indigenous women, so how could he complain? Still, the picture made him feel awful.

"When did this happen?" he asked.

"A few years ago," she said. "Then I had a vision. Like Joan of Arc. Only instead of telling me to learn to ride horses and go save France, my angel said *HIV-positive*!"

"Oh, I'm sorry!" X said, and the jealousy drained away like water. Then he said her name, held badger-tight in the jaws of his memory.

She leaned so close he could hear her breathing behind her bloody mask. "Me too," she whispered. She replaced the picture in her shoe, then slid off the car and picked up a bowl sprinkled with a meager offering of coins. X was almost crying with joy and sadness by this time. He felt his legs weaken, and then her fingers on his arm as she led him to the passenger's side door. He believed if it weren't for those two fingers he might have melted into a puddle and dripped down the gutter to the sewer. She opened the door and he sat down. She walked around and got in behind the wheel.

"You want to be my man again?"

"I do," he said, and slid his mask up. She held his gaze, only her eyes visible through her own mask. Then she shut the door and pulled off her hood and mask, and there appeared her laughing face, glowing in reflected streetlight. Her red hair had begun to gray, and her skin had wrinkled around her eyes and mouth, but still she was beautiful! He held her face between his hands and let flow his tears of joy and grief.

"We could be a team," C was saying. "Forget tonight — this was a bad crowd. Consumers generally pay good money to hear my crap. We could travel around — hit some even bigger religious markets — and I could save you every night, and you could testify to the joys of chastity. We'll rake it in."

X threw his face down onto her lap, smelling her skin through her cape.

"What happened to your businesses?" he mumbled.

"Long story," she said.

"And your bodyguard, did I kill him?"

"Oh no." She started the car. "I married him. He went on to have a long career as a professional wrestler."

X raised C's cape and began kissing her thighs, but paused. "Is this safe?"

She laughed, and squealed the tires as she roared out into street. "Nothing about me has ever been safe!"

X resumed kissing her.

"Brave man," she said, dangling her fingers in his hair.

A twisted tale of heartbreaking pathos, a divine dream, and around the corner another fortuitous encounter

"I'm very ill," C said, smiling enigmatically while she drove. "I'm going to die."

X fought hard to keep back the tears. "Tell me what's happened since I saw you last."

So she began, "After you left with that twitchy bitch —"

"My dear friend," X said.

"Whatever," she said, and waved her hand. "After you left, I married my wounded bodyguard. We had three children, who grew up and moved away, and occasionally send e-mails. Then one day my husband told me he was leaving, too. He said I'd left him unfulfilled. I said, *What?* He said, 'Of course you have, baby. Because if you haven't, then why do I feel as empty as I do?' See, he asked ridiculous questions. He left because we were almost broke."

C paused and took a deep breath. "We'd lost everything to insurance swindlers, internal embezzlers, off-shore banking calamities, taxes, and ungrateful children. The collapse of the shoelace company was just the beginning. I decided I needed a change of scene. I joined an organization of shit-on women, and we went to Africa to help the women learn not to have babies. I wanted to teach birth control, and encourage them to close their legs until their men got off their haunches and did some goddamn work, carried a bucket of water, for instance, or weeded at least one row of yams. Ha!"

"Those sound like good ideas."

"I was a cultural imperialist." She laughed. "Equating *equality* with *justice* is an arbitrary part of *our* culture, not *theirs*. Like in their culture stretching lips and earlobes into outrageous loops is equated with *beauty*."

They'd driven out of the city and were crossing a dark desert. The sky was brilliant with stars.

"It just so happens that watching women carry water and have babies while the men sat around on their haunches offended my recently shit-on woman sensibilities. But hell. The women reproduced. They worked. It's basic. Work and children. The stuff of life. The men? I don't know what they did. Made up myths? Sharpened spears. Occasionally went hunting. I would have been bored. Apparently they weren't. Good for them. Here we are."

They'd arrived at a small oasis where square stucco homes had been built along curving, palm-lined streets. She stopped the car. X followed her across the sandy lawn and stood behind her while she unlocked the front door, opened it, and stepped inside. She held it open for him.

"Nice place," X said, looking around while she flicked a switch and yellow light bathed the room.

"Yeah?" She laughed cynically. "My second husband signed it over to me in the divorce."

"You've been married twice?"

"Briefly and unhappily, if it makes you feel any better."

Actually, it did. X was looking at the photographs on the table of what must be her children. Pictures of their happy baby faces, awkward teen faces, and pictures of their college graduations, each child with flaming red hair, each standing on a beautiful green lawn next to the purple-robed Dr. Fingerdoo. X was going to ask what the doctor was up to, but C pinched his bottom. He jumped. "Ouch!"

She was sunk into a chair behind him, laughing. "My second husband said he was a feminist. I thought that was cool. In fact, I was proud of myself for finding him! And then I realized, I don't know why, but I just realized, maybe watching his smug face eating his third helping of spaghetti, I realized suddenly you can't trust a man who says he's a feminist. Most likely, he's trying to get laid!"

Saying this made her laugh hysterically. While waiting for her to finish, X realized for the first time that in addition to being fatally ill, she might be nuts — which of course is why he'd always loved her.

Suddenly she stood up and her face turned serious. She had something behind her back and she stepped closer. "You still want me?" she whispered, her voice husky and affected.

X didn't answer. He swallowed his terror. She extended the pink tip of her tongue out between her lips and smiled with her eyes. Then she raised her hands from behind her back. One of them held a cowboy hat, which she set on X's head.

"Don't worry," she whispered so her breath touched his ear and made him shiver. "I know countless techniques for preventing the spread of pestilence. Are you ready?"

He wasn't, but he nodded anyway. He felt her cold fingers gently wrap around his wrist. She stepped back and tugged.

"Come this way, my wild man from Borneo," she said. "I want to paint your face."

But there were few nights like this first one. In the weeks and months that followed, C's strength drained rapidly. She never teamed up with X to preach, never moved on to a bigger religious market. It was as if she'd been waiting for somebody to be there before she could weaken and begin to die. X took care of her. Two divorces had left her with no assets but her home, and so when he wasn't cooking for her, bathing her, or washing her sheets, he was replastering the water-damaged bathroom walls, fixing the kitchen plumbing, replacing broken light fixtures, painting the exterior, and generally preparing the house to be sold. When it finally was, they paid the mortgage and back taxes and moved into a two-room apartment. The money they had left for medicine was too little, too late, and she quickly went from bad to worse, growing thinner and thinner before his eyes, her flesh turning her once-beautiful features hideous. Her hair was mostly gone, her face and hands turned to grotesque clumps, and her round bottom caved in on itself. The last to go was the light that slowly dimmed in her eyes.

The morning he discovered her dead, he'd risen early as usual, dressed, and walked into her room to check on her. It was well before dawn and no light shone from behind the drapes, yet even before he turned on a lamp or touched her hand, he knew. Already tired when he woke, he felt the presence of death in the room suck away his last bit of strength and exhaust him to the depths of his bones. He collapsed onto the bed and lay next to her, his face pressed into the thin wisps of hair on the back of her cold head. The sadness in him was deep and still, a part of his cells, and so only slowly did it rise enough to convulse his body in sobs of grief. He'd become an old gray man himself by now, and although he'd been with many women, in many places, it was this one he had always loved. He held the husk of her, felt her skull against his nose, the bones of her shoulders and back against his chest. What a beautiful mystery this had been, the mystery of her, and of loving her. Beautiful for the knowing as well as the unknowing, for the touching as well as for the un-touching. He pressed his teeth into the back of her neck, biting her gently like an old badger, until the tears had passed, and then he let go. He sat up, kissed his fingers, and touched them gently to her shrunken lips.

In the street that morning X passed luridly painted signs hanging over nightspots recently closed. He stepped over men sleeping on the sidewalk and passed shoe shiners squatting outside a church under a pale dawn sky. He paused when the church bells rang and he looked around at the pigeons on the spires and clustered in groups along the sidewalk among hawkers beginning to set up stands.

"What you need, man?" The voice brought him down to earth with a crash. He turned to see a bent old woman laying vegetables on a cloth on the sidewalk.

"I don't know."

"Have a carrot," she said, and handed him one.

X bit the carrot and chewed, immensely grateful. He swallowed and breathed deeply and sat down next to the white-painted trunk of a plastic palm tree. Before the sun rose over the church he'd fallen asleep, and while he slept he dreamed he stood on a rock on the edge of a cliff with his arms spread, face aimed upward at the terrible blue sky.

"WHY?" he shouted.

"BECAUSE!" God said.

The voice of God? He could hardly believe it. He felt immensely grateful and ready to forgive God for everything bad that had ever happened. It didn't even matter that "BECAUSE!" wasn't much of an answer — simply hearing The Voice was enough! X stood on the edge of the cliff and felt tears of joy roll down his cheeks. He savored the tears and he savored the quiver of his lip, and he savored the feeling of immense humility that descended on him and threatened to lower him to his knees. He searched the clear sky in awe of his good fortune. He admired the simplicity of God's response, and he admired the beauty of its authority. Yes. But still he waited. He waited without knowing what he was waiting for. A cool wind had dried his tears, leaving vertical tracks of salt on his face. If God's one word had given him everything he could possibly need — more than any mortal had a right to expect — then why did he once again feel empty? Where had the joy gone so quickly? He felt ashamed and ungrateful but also, now, slightly resentful. If God spoke once, well . . . *then why had He never spoken before?* X stood on the cliff in the sunshine and wind, his feet planted firmly, his eyes open, his chest out, stubborn. After years of earnest and good-faith effort, after too many sleepless nights and days spent looking for the cause of the effect and the effect of the cause, after he'd run out of hope again and again, suffered and survived for years, after wandering from one place to another, living with stupid nagging mysteries such as Why death? Why suffering? Why loneliness? and Why he could sink free throws with his eyes closed on some days and miss the planet on others? after a lifetime of suffering and putting up with too much crap he didn't understand, X figured he deserved a better answer than BECAUSE.

"Because why?" he yelled. He listened to his voice echo off the rock below him and fill the canyon again and again. He listened to his breathing, and he listened to the wind in the trees around him. Had his impatience so infuriated God that God had gone away? He squeezed his eyes shut. He listened. He heard insects buzzing and birds chirping. He thought he heard a helicopter in the distance, and he wondered if it was possible that God was pouting.

"Speak!" X said. "I heareth thee not!"

Heareth-ing himself speak thus, X felt the creep of blood to his face. He wondered if all crazy people felt either proud or ashamed, with no middle ground. He thought thus, for by now he was almost entirely convinced of his own madness. *I am mad*, he thought to himself, thinking perhaps that this might be his only sane thought, and so clinging to it, *I am mad*.

"Because of the tornado!" God said suddenly.

X shuddered. In some countries, crazy people smeared excrement on their skin. In others, crazy people ate dirt. In still others, they walked into public places with guns and shot innocent people. What were the customs of the insane here?

His hands trembled so violently he folded his arms and wedged them against his chest. As carefully as he could he asked, "Because of the tornado, what?"

And God answered: "Because it dropped down like a finger from heaven and it touched the earth. Because it twisted off the crowns of ancient oaks in one shuddering, 250-mile-an-hour yank. Because on that same day 867 children died of starvation in just one East African country; and a bomb blew the limbs off eight passersby on a London street; and the temperature reached 132°F in Tete, Mozambique; and sixteen shoppers at a Tupelo, Mississippi, shopping mall were gunned down by a man carrying a semiautomatic assault rifle and suffering from — what else? — sexual inadequacies; and because a tidal wave drowned 976 people in India; and several regions of southern Russia were being overrun by packs of wolves fleeing the rumbling of gunfire and shelling in the Caucasus; and because large swarms of brown bats gathered in black clouds over Entebbe, polluting water and food supplies with their droppings and causing children to flee as the bats descended on a school compound; and because just the other night in a place you know and love, a giant bubble of carbon dioxide shook loose from the bottom of a crater lake, rose to the surface, and spilled down the side of the volcano, a moving blanket of carbon dioxide gas twenty feet thick that suffocated 2,679 people in valley villages while they slept."

Silence. X heard only the wind in the trees, God's very breath. He heard his own heartbeat. He waited.

"Because," God continued, "because after the tornado in Wonderland it was so quiet and everything was pale and still for days while you and the survivors from town climbed out and picked up, and because after the tornado the countryside swarmed with stray dogs and wandering bands of insurance adjusters, tourists on bicycles, berry pickers with colored headbands, and gypsies looking for old rusty nails they could collect and sell or use as chips in a card game. And because immediately after the tornado passed and you opened your eyes and realized you weren't dead, that exact moment you knew you were alive, you thought of her. And you began looking for her, and you've looked for her your entire life. Even when you were with her you were looking for her, wanting her, closer, always closer. And because although you've always believed you wanted to know why, wanted a cause and effect statement, a description of the world's clinical illness, a phenomenon of some sort, anything with a name, and also because you wanted to know what was around the corner (and also you'd lost your job, too, don't forget that) you hit the road. Do you understand now?"

Before X could answer, he began to wake up from where he slept next to the plastic palm tree. It was already midday and uncomfortably hot, and a familiar voice had replaced God's. The voice spoke words he couldn't understand, words that echoed in his head as though from far away. The speaker grew closer, and the words clearer.

"He did *not* need to be certain," the voice said. "He did *not* need to know how it would end. He did *not* need cause and effect to be clear. Yet he still wanted very much to find a woman for whom he cared deeply."

He opened his eyes, and there in front of him, gazing steadily down at him, stood the woman in pink lamé. Her Betty Boop eyes, shadowed pink, smiled kindly, while her soft hands reached down to help him stand.

"I had a strange dream," he said.

She petted his old head, kissed his cheek.

"Where have you been?" he asked, suddenly full of dreamlike happiness.

Old and gray, her dress mended and altered many times, she gestured to an array of housewares for sale on the sidewalk in front of them.

"Back in retail," she said, "where I've always felt most comfortable. And you?"

X remembered then, and the sadness descended as quickly as it had lifted. "She's dead," he said. "And I need to bury her."

A sad day and a Celebration of Life

In the country where C died, people had a custom that they did not mention the dead. They didn't acknowledge that they themselves would die, or that anybody had ever died. There were no graveyards. Bodies were burned to ashes, and the ashes taken to vast and empty spaces where the wind was encouraged to blow away all traces that the person had ever existed.

Funerals were not called funerals but Celebrations of Life. Speakers discouraged sadness as something to be resisted, as was anger or any other form of insane grief. Life was upbeat, after all, and should be lived happily, and projected images of the departed's smiling, healthy face on a giant screen reinforced this message. The departed "really loved life," the guests were told, which often made them feel ashamed if they currently didn't share the same jolly sentiment.

X and the woman in pink lamé went to a Celebration of Life director to begin this process for C. A lot of money changed hands. C was cremated and her ashes spread over the desert that she'd spent a few miserable nights camping in and "always loved." A ceremony was planned and the director invited Dr. Fingerdoo to speak, which meant even more money changed hands, as Dr. Fingerdoo was now so famous that his agent charged listeners for every sound that came out of his mouth, including burps. All of this money being passed around was good for the Economy, of course, but not so good for X, who'd spent the last of C's house money and now had to borrow from the woman in pink lamé and the recently arrived malformed boy (now an old man).

Still, X couldn't resist nodding his head dumbly to every Celebration of Life feature offered, because — as the director reminded him often — he had loved C very much and surely must want to celebrate her life.

Dr. Fingerdoo, who had shaved his pointy beard and grown million-dollar silver sideburns, began his eulogy by saying winners are part of the solution and losers are part of the problem; winners have a program and losers have an excuse. And to reinforce this point, he used a colorful sports metaphor: winners see a green near every sand trap, and losers see two sand traps near every green!

Then with the projected words VISUALIZE SUCCESS and CELEBRATE LIFE! behind him, he asked the nearly three hundred guests to close their eyes and picture their own success, their own happy life, and the auditorium grew very solemn and quiet. Then the guests were asked to open their eyes and move around the auditorium, to shake hands and form small ad hoc clusters, where they were encouraged "to briefly share their visions."

Finally, with the guests again seated, Dr. Fingerdoo said

that C had lived a good and useful life as a consumer and employer, and generally had made of herself a brilliant economic citizen, earning and spending mucho dinero and doing her multicultural part to expand the Global Free Market.

The guests bobbed their heads in agreement. For a moment, X felt surrounded by many odd little smiling puppets with their heads on springs. He closed his eyes to push away the absurd thought. When he opened them again, a giant colorful image of C's happy, healthy face was being projected onto the screen, and Dr. Fingerdoo was praising an idea she'd whispered to him late one night many years ago when they were both drunk on brandy and the success of the shoestring factory — an idea so outrageous, Dr. Fingerdoo said, as to be pure genius. Her idea was to create systems in which people could buy and sell their very breath. A system in which money would be exchanged with each inhale and exhale. The calculations, kept by a giant supercomputer, would direct huge sums of digital money from one bank account to another, skimming a tiny percentage at the speed of light. Imagine billions of breathers on the earth, each paying to breathe, each getting paid to breathe! Imagine the impact on the Global Free Market! Imagine the spin-off jobs created! Imagine the increase in disposable income that could be spent at Super Stores! Imagine the leap in stock prices, and general prosperity for all, including street children in faraway retail hubs who now must sniff inexpensive glue to drive away hunger pains.

"So as you leave this room," Dr. Fingerdoo concluded, "as you feel your chest expand with breath, remember the miracle of market expansion. And every time you think of the departed, remember too that because of her idea, the market's miraculous value-assessing capacity may someday grow to include the function of your living organs!"

Everybody nodded piously and proudly. What an idea person C had been! What a credit to her multiethnicity! And what an inspirational speaker was Dr. Fingerdoo, who made them feel so good to be alive.

Love, bitterness, and the long trip home

After the Celebration of Life, X, the woman in pink lamé, and the malformed boy, now a malformed old man, chose various transportation modes for the long journey back around the globe to Wonderland. Because none of them had a car, they rode horseback across a bleak and empty landscape dominated by corporate logos emblazoned on hillsides and on the shirts of the peasant inhabitants. In exchange for labor and brand loyalty, competing corporations promised health insurance, retirement benefits, and protection from marauding creditors.

Logo-tattooed knights jousted on hillsides, where mobs of consumers watched and cheered, ready to spend discretionary income with the winner.

Exchanging their horses for covered wagons, the three pilgrims rode in a long wagon train though a dark and superstitious land where their guide warned all virgins to tie themselves in. An economic downturn had caused the locals to get "a little gung ho in the virgin sacrifice department," kidnapping and tossing at least two a week into a local quarry.

At the end of the trail, they filed into buses and then,

near the coast, they joined a commuting crowd on a subway. The train stalled in a tunnel under a river. While our travelers stood patiently gripping handrails in the dark, a squeaky voice leaked from a passenger in the corner.

"Tooooooooo many niggers!" the woman said, unable to resist the anonymity and protection offered by pure darkness.

"Too many whities!" shouted a second voice.

A pause, followed by a third: "Too many Indies and Chinks!"

Then the subway started and the lights came on and the voices ceased. The train pulled out of the tunnel into the bright sunshine of a prosperous and glittering retail hub, where an ethnically diverse group of well-dressed trans-portation consumers disembarked.

At the docks, X, the malformed old man, and the woman in pink lamé caught a ship to cross the ocean. X and the malformed old man wanted to sit out on the deck and look over the vast blue horizon, but the woman in pink lamé insisted on locking herself in her cabin at all times.

"You would too," she said, "if you'd been ravished by forty-two sailors in one night."

So X and the malformed old man settled themselves in chairs on the deck just outside her cabin, and the three of them passed the time by telling each other their long sto-ries through the cracked porthole.

The woman in pink lamé was celebrating thirty years of

sobriety and X was celebrating a lot of years, too, ever since his shoestring factory daze, although he couldn't remember how many.

The malformed old man drank heavily. "Such is the life of an artist," he said. "Be drunken, always drunken!" He raised a glass and drank.

"Why did your head stop moving?" he asked the woman in pink lamé.

"I asked Dr. Fingerdoo that exact question," she said, "and he told me that in the marketplace, when something is taken, something else is given. For example, when a huge hurricane destroys the homes of a thousand people, thousands more people get contracts and jobs to rebuild the homes. So when part of me was involuntarily possessed, another part of me gained a voluntary control."

"Do you believe that?" X asked.

"It's an idea," she said. "One of many out there floating in the marketplace of ideas."

"And how did you get out of the room that day that I had to leave you, before the big earthquake? I came back and you were gone and I've wondered ever since what became of you."

"I don't know," she said. "The effects of trauma are similar to drunkenness. So I don't remember great blocks of what happened for years. Decades. I know as the result of the gang rape I gave birth to twins, a boy and a girl. I know the girl died when she was two or three. I know I mourned her terribly. I know the boy and I traveled around buying and selling whatever we could on the street. I know for a while we fell in with gypsy encyclopedia vendors. They taught us to dance, and they taught my boy to sell encyclopedias to hopeful low-income mothers who couldn't even afford proper food for their children. Being a mother myself, it was not the kind of sales I enjoyed. Soon I left and my boy stayed. He was sixteen, and the gypsies in that country have a good life."

"I hung with some gypsies for a while," said the old malformed man. "Whenever we got to a river or a pond, the women bathed themselves, and their big gypsy breasts bobbed like water lilies on the surface."

There followed a pause in the conversation while all three pilgrims contemplated the image. Then the woman in pink lamé continued, her voice coming through the cracked porthole.

"After my son and I separated, I married, but I have more bad dreams about those years than I do actual memories. I love men dearly but don't enjoy the intimacies, so frankly I made a poor wife. In order to avoid mutual degradation, he finally left me, the dear, and I found myself alone on the streets of a distant city, a strange place where the inhabitants measured their worth in aluminum coins made with foil mined from ancient landfills. I didn't know how I got there, or why a stranger was kind to me, and took me in, and for months fed me all the french fries I could eat. It was then I realized I was still alive, after all my losses. Still alive and still sober, and growing plump again!"

Moved by her story, X said, "I wish I could tell you how

often I wondered about you. That empty hotel room haunted me for years."

"And I about you," she said. "In fact, when I saw you sleeping against the plastic tree, I remembered your sad face the first night I saw you and I felt a tenderness I had not felt in decades. I knew just what to say."

The malformed old man, who was well drunk by now, couldn't stand it anymore. "I hate this love talk," he said. "Why don't you two just get it over with."

The woman in pink lamé answered through the porthole. "Because we're platonic lovers," she said.

"*Platonic*," the malformed old man mocked, and swigged from his drink. "You mean *pathetic*?"

"Why are you so bitter?" the woman in pink lamé asked.

"Don't knock bitterness," he said. "It's all I have left!" Then he told how one night, in the paradise valley where he and X had lived, and where he'd found happiness painting penises on houses, one night a nearby volcano burped and a huge cloud of poisonous gas slid down the mountain slope to the village, where it settled and suffocated every man, woman, and child! He said by chance he was traveling and so he wasn't there, otherwise he'd be dead like his thirteen wives and four dozen children. He said since then he'd been drunk and bitter, and if they didn't mind (and even if they did), he figured he'd stay that way.

When X heard the story he felt a cold lump in his stomach and his face turned ashen. "I dreamed about that volcano," he said.

"Well, be grateful you didn't live it," the malformed old man said, knocking back his drink and refilling his glass from the open bottle on the deck next to his chair. "Imagine walking into a village where everyone you love is dead."

X tried but the horror was too great.

"That's very sad," the woman in pink lamé said. "But I'll just briefly point out that even when you were young and had everything, back when we first met, you were full of bitterness and scorn. Those are two things that life has *not* knocked out of you."

The malformed old man smiled drunkenly, and burped.

Old life in a new world, or the other way around

They arrived back on the shores of Wonderland the next morning, and in the days that followed they made their way by bus across their homeland. After having been gone for decades, what X noticed most was how his countrymen surrounded themselves with machines. In fact, it was a rare moment when a Wonderlandian was not using a machine or talking about one. Machines to work and play more efficiently. To wake, to move, to buy, to sell, to plant, to harvest, and to tell stories more efficiently. To heat and to cool. To build and destroy, to slice and cook and clean. To facilitate, obfuscate, educate, communicate, procreate and even, in the back of the bus at night, to masturbate.

Machines that hummed and buzzed and pounded and roared. Machines that went BANG BANG BANG! or *ping ping ping* or Ker-*BLAM*! Machines that zoomed and groaned and hissed. Machines that combined to make a low, unending moan across the land.

On the evenings they stayed in motels, X would walk outside after the others had gone to bed. He'd stand under the streetlights or stars and still hear the machines, near and far and in all directions. Cars and trucks and trains and planes and irrigation pumps and forced air vents, mowers, blowers, a phone ringing, and a radio playing the same song or news or talk-radio show all across the country. One voice, one efficient marketing system, one machine noise ubiquitous as the sound of a rooster's crow in darker, poorer lands.

When they arrived in their hometown they recognized nothing. Not one street, not one building, not one tree. During their absence, vermiculite had been discovered in one of the hills nearby and so a mine had been built and then a plant to process the vermiculite into asbestos. There had been work in the mines and work at the plant, and work driving trucks back and forth from the mine to the plant. The asbestos was used to insulate houses, and to lighten the soil in the garden, and to pave the high-school running track, and to fill sandboxes, and everybody was happy for about twenty years until thousands began to get sick with lung disease. So all the buildings were torn down, and the topsoil hauled away, and there was new work building new houses on the bedrock, and there was new work taking care of the sick and burying the dead, and also in public relations creating a new image for the town that "downplayed" the toxic history.

Super Stores were built to give all the busy consumers a place to spend their new money, and some of them worked in the Super Stores, and some planted seedlings on bald and eroding hillsides where the trees had been cut to make wood for the new homes. The climate had changed and the summers were hotter and more humid, and so to avoid unpleasant perspiration people stayed inside their air-conditioned homes and watched TV shows about lightly employed, quirky young people with great sex lives who have wacky shopping adventures in distant cities, or shows about cops in those same cities who risk their lives every day to keep the streets clean of scumbag low-income people, or heartless rich people who might interfere with all of the caring and optimistic young buffed cleavagey shoppers.

Sometimes they changed the channel and watched the patriotic war Wonderlandian troops were fighting far away to keep the market free, a war against mean people who just plain "didn't get it," economy- or cultural-wise, and weren't as good at making weapons, either. Wonderlandian bombs hit perfectly, which made for clean consciences and high ratings, and even more money for the news companies, in which many of the viewers held stock.

"Everything has changed and nothing has," X said.

"You have fewer teeth," the malformed old man said, "and my body is bent and broken, and hardened in this misshaped form, and the woman in pink lamé's head has stopped moving, and her dress is ragged, and her hair is gray, and I can't get a hard-on very often, and since your lover died you don't seem to want one, and the woman in pink lamé is afraid of one and —"

"All right already," said the woman in pink lamé. "We get it."

The three of them moved into a faux-colonial cottage in the country, and the woman in pink lamé got work in a Goat Cheese Super Store, fifteen acres of different varieties of goat cheese, located in the nearest retail hub between the Grease Zirc Super Store and the Upbeat-Art Super Store. Drivers of automobiles that fouled the air came to shop, and drivers of automobiles who worked on building automobiles that didn't foul the air came to shop, and people who'd lost everything in the flooding on the coast came to shop with their insurance money, and insurance people who were charging higher flood-insurance premiums came to shop, and builders who were getting the insurance money to rebuild came to shop, and the cyanide mine workers came to shop with the eco-cleanup workers. C and Dr. Fingerdoo's theory of paying for the inhale and selling the exhale seemed to be playing out, at least in fair Wonderland, where bank accounts continued to bulge with electronic money transferred back and forth between bank computers. Everybody sent their children to schools to teach them how to be good consumers, and how to figure out what they could sell and how to sell it, what to foul and how to clean it up again.

Because of what management called his "high cultural awareness," and because he could speak to many of the workers in their native languages, X got work in an egg factory hiring and overseeing laborers, making certain everybody got four bathroom and fresh air breaks per shift. Everybody except the laying hens, of course, who passed their brief span piled together with a half-dozen other hens in a wire cage whose floor a single magazine page could carpet, which led to a range of behavioral "vices" that might include cannibalizing cagemates or rubbing their bodies against the wire mesh until they were featherless and bleeding. And when the hens' output began to ebb, they were starved of food and water and light for several days in order to stimulate a final bout of egg laying before death.

Thanks to the efficient system, and to the efforts of the multiethnic workforce, and of course to the hens, X was able to save enough money to quit the egg factory job and start a small business as a deck-building consultant. *Decks Unlimited*, said the Yellow Pages ad. *Why pull your chair out on the lawn, when you can pull it out onto a new deck?*

The malformed old man traveled a lot selling paintings of giant, multicolored vulvas, alone or in gardens. Sometimes he had to travel to far-off corners of the world — *connections, the game was in connections* — but often he'd be home and they'd all sit outside and eat breakfast at dawn together. He'd wear his old Cleveland Indians cap, and the woman in pink lamé would tease him, and X would marvel at how much the same they were as on that first sad unemployed night they'd met — the same but different, too.

Sometimes as X watched the sun break pretty and pink over the horizon and he felt the change of seasons in his very old bones, he tried in vain to reconcile the beauty of the planet with the common misery of its inhabitants. He remembered the tortured prisoners, dead factory workers, lines of hungry job seekers, twisted bodies crushed under rubble, bloody soldiers and burned-to-a-crisp indigenous peoples, production unit chickens and C's precious diseased body, and for the life of him he could not comprehend how all of that painful experience had led to this new and final comfort. The mystery was too big for him. He could no more name the source of his sadness than he could the object of his immense gratitude.

The malformed old man drank gin and orange juice, X sipped tonic water, and the woman in pink lamé drank cranberry juice cocktail.

"Think of it this way," the woman in pink lamé would say when she felt them growing distant and sad. "The world is much older than any of us, and it'll be around a lot longer, too."

"So what?" asked the malformed old man.

"So imagine we are three old peasants sitting around during medieval times feeling bad because the dukes and knights and kings and queens and popes have messed everything up."

X laughed.

"Here's to luscious serving wenches!" said the malformed old man, lifting his glass of gin.

"But those three old peasants couldn't change the feudal system," the woman in pink lamé said, "any more than we can change the system now. The world has to grow out of itself. There has to be the equivalent of the Black Death and huge technological advances in shipbuilding. Is Dr. Fingerdoo right? Is the Global Free Market divine? We'll never know! All we know is that the world blows through our lives like a big wind, sometimes fair and sometimes foul. It lifts and flaps us like sheets on a line, and our one true choice is to hang on or not, and so far we have. We've made it to where we are, however we've done it, and all we can do is remember those good people we knew who, despite their best efforts, blew away in a big gust or shredded in a gale. And all we can hope is to be fondly remembered."

There followed after her speech a long silence while the three of them considered their past losses and future deaths, but before they grew too melancholy the woman in pink lamé took X's hand and the gnarled fingers of the malformed old man. The yellow sun had risen into a pale blue sky and colored green the round western hills.

"Finish up now," she said, gently squeezing their hands. "It's time to go to work."